LEGACY

OR

LOVE

WILLIAM D. COUGHLAN

Coughlan and Associates Publishing

USA

A COUGHLAN AND ASSOCIATES PUBLICATION

Coughlan and Associates specialize in consulting, publishing, personal development, strategic planning and visioning for individuals and groups, as well as leadership and management issues.

Coughlan and Associates Publishing
P.O. Box 6625
Columbia, MD 21045
E-mail: wcoughlan @ home.com
877-850-4938

ISBN 0-9678341-0-4
Publishers Cataloguing In Publication
Coughlan, William D.
  Legacy or Love/William D. Coughlan. - -1st ed.
  p.cm.
  Includes bibliographical references and index.
  ISBN: 0-9678341-0-4

  1. Love stories, American. 2. Self-realization - -
Fiction. 3. Success- - Fiction. I. Title.

PS3553.O795L44 2000   813'.6
                    QBI00-900204

Printed in the United States of America

To all those who love passionately

and make their life and their legacy

a legacy of love

ACKNOWLEDGMENTS

Inspiration has come from many.

Obviously I am thankful to my parents, Thomas Eugene Coughlan and Helen Mildred Coughlan for having me. Thanks also to their parents and especially Lady Helen Lamalle who was a unique personal and professional inspiration.

Next my thanks to Sue, my wife, who has nurtured our children, grandchildren, other friends, orphans and strays that may have come our way. Her parents John Moran and especially Dorothy Ann Lang gave us much.

Thanks also to my three brothers, T.J., Dick and Terry, who like ideal siblings, always loved, encouraged and were supportive. They, like me, were unconditionally loved by wonderful parents, spouses, family members and good friends.

Each of our children Willie Sean, Richard Shannon, Michael Shane, Kristin Ann, Suzi Danielle, and Joseph Thomas have always inspired me and pushed me to try to be better.

We have been graced by Brittany Kaya, Anthony Jordan, and Sean Christopher, some in the oven and I know there will be others. Thanks to Kenny Porter, Jerome Taylor, Lara and Heather who have expanded our legacy.

Thanks to my teachers, mentors and role models, too many to list.

Thanks to the publishing team, Kristin Taylor, Catherine Farrell, Jill Kamin, Carol Bittner, Mary Van Dyke and Madlyn Darnell Stewart, the typists, and Roxanne Shenker, publishers assistant.

Special thanks to Sandra Yeyati, editor, Pen Pal, Marianne Gischler, editor, Tracy Kiernan, cover designer, Gulf Coast Media and Sam Arcure, Plaza Photo, all of Naples.

Thanks also to the staffs of Collier County Library, Florida Gulf Coast University and Kinko's, especially Jane Whiddon and Maryann Mueller.

Special thanks to all those who have graced me with their presence, inspired, laughed, cried, loved and searched with me. I will be forever grateful.

PREFACE

Life, like our love and our legacy, has great meaning for us. If we are open to it.

In this story what do I mean by legacy or love?

By legacy I mean the gift, the remembrance, the value left with or handed down to others by ourself. It is the substantial impact and effect we have on others, hopefully more positive than negative.

By love, I mean the passionate and devoted affection we communicate in our fondness and cherishing of ourself, of others and our life. It is the beloved, kind and endearing attitude; a deep feeling; and the most virtuous, immaculate, elegant and decent feeling we can convey in our everyday life. It is the boundless, everlasting, sacred and most powerful emotion on earth radiating in our glorious presence. It is the greatest word in our vocabulary.

By focusing more on the seriousness of life as well as fun, we can achieve greater love in our life and leave a rich and more endearing legacy for others, if we so choose.

Oftentimes our life choices and priorities prevent us from creating love and a valuable legacy.

By reflecting on our love and our legacy, we can live more passionately and be happier, more responsible and truthful in our daily interaction with others including our lovers. We can create richer lives by being more respectful, visioning our future, and also learning life's lessons. We can experience the flow of love if we re-evaluate our desires for love and create a more valuable personal legacy.

I have some suggestions.

Read this book. Then read it again, reflecting on how it might apply to your own life... its past, present and future. Think about your past and current love(s). Reflect on your current and future legacy. Focus on your desired loves and legacy. Think about yourself passionately! Who are you? Who do you want to be? I believe we have fantastic opportunity to enjoy even richer lives than that which we already take for granted.

I wrote this book to create a story about two successful people, like you, who have achieved much in life and their loves. They have created legacies of immense magnitude. They are not perfect. In fact, because they are attractive, successful and influential, they are subject to greater challenges and expectations. These challenges concern deep values and strong passions, such as love, responsibility, human potential, truth, respect, and lifelong learning, all of which have great impact in our daily living.

May you enjoy this love story as it unfolds within their families, their interesting professional lives and their circle of talented friends and colleagues in Washington, D.C., Northern Virginia, Maryland and Colorado - where they vacation.

May it help you to reflect upon your own rich life, and your loves and your legacy. May it help you in your role as principal author and interior designer of your ever- richer love life and fulfilling legacy.

FOREWORD

I have traveled many places and met many fascinating and stimulating people.

I have also written several books relating to my travel and those interesting people I met.

Throughout the world Washington, D.C. is revered for its powerful and captivating people.

In Legacy or Love, Bill Coughlan has captured the essence and power of not only Washington, D.C., but also of some of the characters in that city. Legacy or Love is a must-read for those interested in an insightful story about successful people, like you, who are concerned with their legacy and their love regardless of where they travel or where they live.

Bob Johnston
Author of Living Overseas; What You Need to Know
Living Overseas; Mexico
Living Overseas; Costa Rica

Chapter 1
Live Passionately

"I'm glad that's over!" stated Danielle.

"Your marriage or your taxes?" asked her friend Cathryn.

"My taxes of course."

"I thought you meant your marriage."

"You're not serious?"

"I am. After thinking about how you ignore him. Take him for granted. I thought for sure you meant Robert."

"Robert loves me."

"I know he does. The question is do you love him and how much?"

"I love him very much," Danielle vehemently responded. "We've been deeply in love for years."

"Then why don't you show that love more?"

"Cathryn!"

"Well?"

"What makes you say such things?"

"You are the one who said 'I'm glad it's over.'"

"I had just sealed my IRS envelope!"

"How was I to know it wasn't a letter to Robert telling him it was over?" A slight grin formed on one side of Cathryn's mouth.

"You jump to such hasty conclusions. I am amazed, especially coming from you, such a bright woman and my best friend."

"Really, Danielle, how much do you love Robert?" Cathryn's grin disappeared.

"Why are you pushing this question, Cathryn?"

"Because you are acting very differently lately and I don't

understand it, nor do others. I am sure Robert is concerned."

"Robert is not concerned."

"See, you are admitting that there's something for Robert to be concerned about. Now tell me... what is going on in your life?"

"Nothing is going on. I mean nothing regarding Robert and me."

"Or any other man in your life?"

After hesitating briefly, "Or with any other man in my life."

"Danielle, I question that."

"Well, question it. You are always questioning things. That is one of the interesting and redeeming features of your personality, Cathryn."

"You are just changing the subject."

"No, I am not. Just complimenting you on your intelligence."

"Danielle, this is getting a little heavy. Let's order lunch." Cathryn motioned to the waiter, who approached their table.

"I'll have the pasta Italiano Supremo," said Danielle.

Turning toward the waiter, Cathryn said, "I'll have your seafood special."

"May I suggest a wine?" asked the waiter.

"Sure."

"We've got a very nice California Zinfandel in from the Napa Valley."

"Excellent," responded the women, both dreaming of the wines they tasted in many different cities across the country, not to mention the wines of Paris, Venice, Hong Kong and Sydney.

"Isn't spring wonderful?" asked Cathryn.

"You know, I was thinking the same thing," said Danielle.

"It is one of my favorite times in Washington, D.C. Along with the early fall, of course."

"I met one of the most fascinating policy analysts last night, " stated Cathryn.

"Oh really, who was he?"

"His name is Franklin Dickinson."

"Sounds like an historic family from the Main Line in Pennsylvania. Is he related to Benjamin Franklin?"

"You know that's funny that you would say that, Danielle. Because I thought the same thing right after meeting him."

"Well, is he?"

"I don't know. But I'm going to find out."

"Why, will you see him again soon?"

"Nothing scheduled, but we'll see," remarked Cathryn, sporting a mischievous smile.

"I'm sure you will. By the way, how's Richard?"

"Mr. Livingston is quite well, thank you, as are our two children. Danielle, let me ask you. With it being spring and all, have you given any more thought to having children, with Robert of course?"

"Sometimes."

"Sometimes? Well how often recently?" Cathryn asked.

"I don't know. From time to time."

"Well, unless you are going to adopt children when you are in your late forties and fifties, I suggest you seriously decide now. You are 39 years old, Executive Director for the Women's Health Caucus. And who knows, regardless of how health reform goes this year, it could be all over for the legislation or there may be an even greater need for your group. You are not getting any younger. And besides, I know you have accomplished an awful lot already, but more than likely if you aren't up to miracles, now is the time to decide. Maybe that's what you've been discussing with another man."

"Why are you still inquiring about Robert and me? If I have a baby, it will be with Robert," said Danielle.

"Will it?"

"Yes."

"Let me ask you another thing. What really moves you? I mean, here you are: a brilliant, attractive CEO. Your education and professional background has been unique. Who else do you know has a Master's in Fine Arts from a leading theatre school in Chicago, Goodman, with a joint curriculum from DePaul University's Philosophy Department, who then gets an MBA from George Washington University and has an extensive background in government relations and the health industry?"

"I don't know of too many."

"Exactly. In a lot of ways you've had it all."

"Well, remember, I considered getting a Ph.D. from the well-respected University of Southern California's Public Affairs School."

"Well that's what I mean, do you want to be a professional politician, corporate CEO, writer, producer, or what? Danielle, you could do it all."

"Maybe I already have."

"Maybe."

"Very funny. I don't plan to die at 39."

"Oh, no? Well then, when?"

"I don't know. That's sort of a crazy question. One minute you're telling me I ought to have children and the next you're anticipating my ensuing death!"

They both laughed heartily.

"You know, Cathryn, I really enjoy having lunch with

4

you."

"I'm serious, Danielle, you have tremendous potential, and you have accomplished a lot. But like a lot of us, you better clarify what your real values and passions are."

"I know what my values and passions are. I live them."

"I know you do. So do I. That's why we enjoy each other's company. But where are we as we contemplate this beautiful April day? Where are we and where are we going?"

"Oh Cathryn, you are a trip. Sometimes I wonder if you are my conscience, or I am yours. You've shared very little during this lunch regarding yourself. You have been a successful financial consultant to the International Monetary Fund, the World Bank, and other international financial interests. You've traveled the world extensively, far more than me, though you and I have shared many stories in many different places. You are the Superwoman of today. Two wonderful children. And now, like me, an association executive director and CEO of an international services association. How about you? What are your real values and passions?"

"I'm fine. Listen, you are the one who called and said let's have lunch. It's springtime. Isn't it a great time to talk and dream? So I'm asking you, what are you dreaming, Danielle?"

"Well, you're right, Cathryn. I've been dreaming a lot lately. And not just about what taxes Robert and I owe. Taxes take almost 40 percent of what we earn. There is definitely more to life than making a buck. But you and I have discussed this before. And we have lived our lives accordingly."

"Yes, but Danielle, recently I have noticed you acting, I don't know, more creatively. Like you're testing the limits of time or of society. Maybe it's the fact that you're nearing forty and reevaluating your entire life. That's great. It is just that you are acting very differently, and I've known you for, what, twelve or thirteen years, since we worked for the federal government in government relations activities?"

"Isn't the dressing on these salads out of this world?"

"Yes it is superb. Are you going to answer my question or avoid it?"

"I'll hit it right on, Cathryn. Yes, I am reevaluating my entire life. Yes, I am very happy. Yes, I am wondering about having children. But I am really trying to put it all in perspective. Have I carefully analyzed all that is going on with me? How I feel? How my emotions are moving me? What I am doing professionally and personally? What does my family mean to me? Robert? My parents? You? My sisters? My other friends? I love what I do. Yes, like this national health care reform debate, it has really been frustrating. With insurance self-interests, corporate self-interests, the self-interest and narrow views of the small business sector, not to consider medical, hospital, other allied health and various government concerns, it has been a confusing mess with seemingly little concern about addressing those who need health insurance and don't have it, and addressing the cost concerns that are still pressing, and this is all after the Balanced Budget Act took one hundred and fifteen billion dollars out of Medicare!"

"Well, so is that why you are so frustrated with the world conditions from the oven of health care reform, that maybe you are burned out, Danielle."

"Well, maybe, but I guess I don't like to admit to burnout. I am 39. I exercise approximately three to four times a week with aerobics and other exercise. I feel good. I am successful professionally, yet feel there is much more to accomplish to make this earth a better place."

"Danielle, I applaud you and know you have done a lot through your volunteer efforts professionally and personally, as well as through every professional hour, day in, day out. But what specifically are you dreaming or what do you want to do about it?"

"I think I'm going to have to reflect further on it before I lay it all out before you. I do know that I am wrestling with all kinds of priorities and passions like never before. And I don't think it is just because I am nearing forty. I am wrestling with devoting more time to Robert, to a new baby, to achieving something never before accomplished in health reform, helping others to realize more compassion in the world or making a greater contribution to this earth and people on this earth, to mastering a greater balance in my life and the lives of others regarding our personal lives, our family lives and professional lives."

"Danielle, I love you. You always order up a great and magnificent menu for the entire world order. Maybe you just need to relax, take it a bit lighter and have a bit more fun. You know this town is wonderful. It has more power per block than any in the world. But let's not allow the craziness of Washington, D.C. to consume us."

"You are right Cathryn. But there are many issues that you and I both face and must clarify to find total happiness. You and I have talked about this before, and we'll definitely talk about it again. We can help each other, our loved ones and others like never before. And I believe that there is a new and different clarification of those values and those principles that really haven't been laid out and accepted by the masses. I hope to do that for people in Washington, D.C., this country and around the globe."

"That's terrific, Danielle. What luscious thing should we get for dessert? And I don't mean who is sitting in this restaurant or walking Pennsylvania Avenue. I mean on this great dessert tray."

*   *   *

It was May in Washington, D.C. A simply beautiful month with the cherry blossoms turning gorgeous. Danielle had been quite busy the last couple of weeks. Health care reform was no less a frustrating issue than before. And Danielle knew that, for the coming five to six months, it would not change. With the way Congress was acting and various self interests, principally the insurance industry and the small business sector, it was unclear whether something significant regarding health care reform was going to pass and be signed by the President. It was hard to find the champions for the cause.

Fortunately for Danielle, she and Robert were having a good time, and Danielle's older sister was to visit. Maria, an elementary school teacher, was married with two children and, like Danielle, possessed a master's degree but hers was in elementary education. They shared many similar life perspectives, except Danielle had always been more of a risk taker and may have accomplished more professionally, although both had been successful.

Obviously, with her Washington, D.C. background, Danielle was a little more worldly.

Danielle walked through National Airport to the gate where her sister was supposed to arrive. As she walked, Danielle reminisced about Maria as well as about her younger sister Lisa, who was the more traditional homemaker with a high school degree and four children aged three to twelve.

Danielle also thought about her mother and father, now ages sixty-one and sixty-six respectively, Ann and John DiCarlo. Danielle's father John was the most accomplished politician in Chicago and Illinois. He was a state senator for twenty years between the ages of 27 and 47. He had been majority leader in the Illinois State Senate for four years before retiring to pursue insurance and real estate development interests, in Chicago and the nearby South and Southwest suburbs. He had given Danielle her strong political orientation and served as an ideal political role model for Danielle as a teenager, who often accompanied her father to political events in the Chicago area. John was close to the late Michael K. Ryan, former mayor of Chicago for decades. He was also close to many Governors of Illinois.

Ann Newman DiCarlo was a very good mother, spending most of her time raising the three DiCarlo sisters while helping John in any way possible. Ann was a physical therapist by professional training who practiced part time and had always been involved in social welfare activities, especially related to children and teenagers. She had recently been appointed to a State Commission on Crime Prevention in Illinois because of her volunteer crime prevention activities with the school system.

The public announcement system at National Airport said the American flight from Chicago would be on the ground shortly. As Danielle waited, she saw Senator Twetchell of Nebraska, and Danielle thought how he would be retiring from his Senate Majority Leader position this year. President Diane Jackson would miss his insightful reassuring counsel next year, Danielle thought. She then started wondering if Senator Twetchell, rumored to be married, would in fact be married and have children. If Senator Twetchell and his wife had children, perhaps Robert and she should have children after all. She would have to inquire about Maria's children and how they were doing when she got off the plane.

As she waited for her sister Maria to arrive, Danielle thought her sister was a model of legacy and love. Danielle, Maria and their other sister Lisa were fortunate to have been born in a good family with loving parents. Their mother and father had emphasized from an early age for the girls to be loving people. That was what was most important in life.

They had learned as soon as they were able to comprehend that everyone is driven by legacy or love. Or perhaps a legacy of love. Legacy meant the gift, the remembrance, the value left with or handed down from person to person, generation to generation. It was the substantial impact and effect one had on others, hopefully one that was more positive than negative.

Love meant the passionate and devoted affection communicated between people reflecting their fondness, respect and deepest liking for each other and for life. It was a beloved, kind and endearing attitude, a deep feeling and the greatest emotion shared in their lives.

At least that is what Danielle DiCarlo's family firmly believed. It was their task to share that belief and feeling and teach it to the world.

Each of their parents, in their own unique way, had emphasized the purpose and meaning of life. It was simple, to love and be loved because you were a loving being, first and foremost. The concern from the beginning was with one's own legacy, to be a good person and help others to achieve their full potential as loving persons.

There were so many people on earth who had not been

loved as children or as adults. They had not experienced what love and life was all about. But Danielle, Maria and their sister Lisa had experienced it in their mother's womb and from the time they were born into this world. Indeed, they were fortunate. Their responsibility and their purpose was to return that love to parents, family members and everyone else they met. As Christ had said, so did their mother and father, "love one another as I have loved you."

Their individual legacies might be realized, experienced and witnessed in different ways. But at the core of their being, the core of their legacy was to love. And as much as Danielle thought her sister, in her modest yet authentic way, was the epitome of legacy and love, perhaps the most was expected of Danielle, a woman of much promise and many talents. And she was viewed as beautiful by practically everyone who encountered her.

Just then, her sister Maria stepped off the plane.

"Maria, how are you?" Danielle said as her sister rushed towards her. They hugged. Hugs had always been cherished in the DiCarlo household.

"Danielle, great to see you," responded Maria, as she warmly embraced the sister she idolized and loved.

"Great to see you and be with you," Danielle replied.

"How's our Washington connection?"

"Did Pa tell you to say that?"

"How did you guess?"

"Pa is always riding me, asking me when I'm going to get appointed to the Administration."

"Not the best time for that is it?" asked Maria.

"When is the best time? I was approached about one position. Wasn't exactly what I was interested in and I didn't want to give up my position in health reform unless it was something significant. Enough about me. How are you doing?"

"Great. Although I was looking forward to this weekend trip to see you. Especially after Mom remarked that she really thought there was something going on with you and Robert."

"What do you mean?" said Danielle, with concern reflected in her forehead.

"Oh you know Mom. Whenever she asks you about Robert she thinks you are curt with your response."

"Well, I usually say he's fine and that's it, because it is fine between us."

"I don't know what Mom is implying. I'm merely sharing with you confidentially what Mom has said to me."

"Well, I appreciate that, but you can share with her that she need not be concerned about Robert and me."

"Okay, I will," said Maria.

"So Maria, how are the children?"

"The kids are great. Joseph is in the fifth grade. He is such a happy boy. He's never been a problem."

"Wait till he's a teenager."

"Yeah, I know that's what everybody says. At least I have three more years of bliss."

"And Patsi, how is she doing?"

"Good. You know she's a girl. We all have our developmental challenges. Actually she's doing quite well. Last year in the second grade, she didn't seem to care whether she excelled or failed in school. I thought she was reverting to her terrible twos."

"My goodness, Maria, you should count your blessings. Here she is only in the third grade now and she's expressing such emotions and passion for living. You and I see too many people who just live in the everyday world, express little emotion, and live in the gray twilight that knows not the joy of victory and the agony of defeat. That's one thing Pa gave us girls. Always strive to live, to win, to learn to better oneself and to better the lot for all people."

"I know, Danielle, I think about that often as we rise and fall with how Patsi does on this test or that, or whether she's doing well in soccer that day or not. You know how meaningful all those daily reactions were when you were eight years old. Or do you remember back that far?"

"Stop it, Maria. Everyone has been bugging me about turning 40."

"Well, you are getting up there."

"Really, Maria. Yes, I remember when I was eight and you were six. And I remember when you became eight."

"What do you recall?"

"Mom and Pa were very spiritual."

"I know."

"They delayed us from receiving our first Holy Communion until we were eight years old. Pa was quite determined about that. I remember him telling the sister at school that he wanted us to truly appreciate what we were receiving, that it was the bread of life, the gift of everyday life. And he thought us waiting from age seven to age eight would give us that keener appreciation of life as symbolized in the body and blood of Christ through first Holy Communion."

"I remember the same thing, Danielle, and fondly. He was right."

"Yes, he was right. And you know what else I remember? Wait a minute. There's my car over there."

"Wow, when did you get a red Mercedes convertible?"

13

"Oh, last summer. It is a year old."

"Wow, it looks brand new. I, of course, have my little Ford Escort and Anthony has the four-door Chevy Impala, you know the all-American family. Not like Dr. and Mrs. Washington, D.C.!"

"Stop it, Maria. Cars aren't everything and you know that."

"Then why the Mercedes?"

"I don't know, I just liked it. It jumped out at me. I had a passion for it. Where were we? Oh yes back when we were eight years old. But you know what else I remember about Pa?"

"What?"

"He made us wonder, transcend the everyday life. Remember how often we would go to the zoo and Pa would point out interesting and insightful things about each of the animals and their ways."

"Yes, from the mischievous monkeys and their creative ways to the majestic lions and their powerful stares and deliberate walks."

"I have to laugh. It is those insights that have helped me deal with the characters here in Washington and their illusions of power and gamesmanship."

"You know, those were powerful personal insights that we gained. And Ma with her compassion for all human beings. Whether it was the ones she was rehabbing or the other kids in trouble she would help, we really learned what was important in life."

"You know, Maria, how Pa would talk about our visions, and how he would have to vision our family life and we would have to vision our personal life. He was and is a man ahead of his times. He should have been Mayor of Chicago or Governor of

Illinois."

"He was majority leader of the Senate in Illinois. Don't you think that is a powerful position?"

"Yes of course. I just mean he could have influenced so many lives in a positive way."

"God, Danielle, he did. He influenced you and me and our sister Lisa. Plus all those he came in contact with in Illinois politics, and he had contacts nationally through the National Conference of State Legislators. My goodness. Plus all those in our neighborhood, in Chicago, in the suburbs. I mean Pa has had some very positive impacts on a lot of people."

"I realize that. I also know, as you stated, that Ma instilled in us that spiritual dimension toward the sacredness of life, to be able to listen to others, to truly understand them, and to realize the real value of human life."

"As we stated before, life in all of its aspects, whether at the zoo, or do you remember when Ma and Pa would take us out to Palos Heights and we would walk among nature and climb the hills and picnic there? That was fun."

"Yes... and exhilarating. It helped us gain a personal insight into the family and all its dimensions. It touched and expanded the spiritual, physical, mental and social aspects of our being."

"Oh, now you're getting philosophical. I feel the Goodman Theatre dramatist and DePaul philosophies in you coming out, Danielle."

"But it is true, we learned to find balance and value in life at early ages and that was reinforced as it should be. We are very lucky girls."

"I know. I think about it often. Especially when I realize there are so many people stressed out, burned out and very

15

cynical and negative about what is going on with their own lives, those of their families and those in the world. Danielle, I need to tell you of this one teacher at school. She is such a negative influence on the children and other teachers. She should not be teaching. She's been divorced twice, mid-thirties, hates men, doesn't really care for her own children, shuffles them back and forth between her ex-husbands, ex-husband's families and her own families. I mean it is a circus. She doesn't care for those kids. She doesn't love or even care much for herself. She is very disillusioned about life, about herself and everyone connected to it."

"That is why it helps to get involved in professional groups. Of course, you and I have had numerous positive role models in our personal lives. But professionally I have found positive insights from affiliations in associations. For me it meant serving on the Board of Directors of prestigious groups like the Greater Washington Society of Association Executives and the American Society of Association Executives. It is why I have my staff that plan our meetings around the country involved in such helpful groups as the   Professional Convention Management Association and Meeting Planners International. Many working people don't take advantage of such associations, which can enlighten and re-energize their skills and talents."

"I know Danielle. I have done similarly with my professional education associations. They helped me realize my value and potential in a positive way, unlike that narrow-minded, negative teacher I was describing."

"I can multiply those negative personalities many times in this town. Everybody thinks they are a big deal because they work for Senator so and so or in the White House. Or because they have achieved this legislative accomplishment as a lobbyist or have been able to modify a significant regulation affecting their industry. But you and I would not want to have lunch with them or even spend time with them. They are power mongers, unbalanced personalities who need to get a life. Believe me, Maria, these people, like many you and I deal with in our daily lives, need to find balance in their personal, family and professional lives."

"Well, Danielle, I see where Ma and Pa accomplished something with us. They gave us basic skills and human insights. Plus the ability to be positive and help others. We are indeed fortunate."

"Remember the sign Ma had in the kitchen that said we have the power to choose whether the next minute will be sixty seconds of happiness or sixty seconds of negative thought."

"Yes I do and it is still in the kitchen."

"Maria, with change all around us, the increased use of technology and computers and everything happening quicker, people are not able to adapt, to survive, much less thrive in their own lives and those they are connected with."

"That's the problem, Danielle, they are not connected to others."

"That's true, Maria. There is more divorce, more orphaned children, more jobs that are simply jobs, more managers in your educational field, my health fields and in the corporate world, that are simply going through the motions in their everyday lives. Why don't they stop and reflect on their life and value the joy of it?"

"Maybe because they never enjoyed our family life. A family with close siblings like the three of us, a loving and devoted mother and father, close cousins, aunts, uncles and grandparents."

Danielle drove out of National Airport onto the George Washington Parkway. "By the way," Danielle inquired "how are Gramps and Gram?"

"Oh, they are great as always. Gramps tells stories like he always did. He's a stitch at 86."

"Is that how old he is? He's remarkable."

"He is. You should see Gram."

"Yeah, I talked to her by phone last week," said Danielle.

"But you should see her live and in color, and I mean in color. Last month she was working in that garden of hers full of flowers and vegetables. It looks like the rainbow. Beautiful colors. She was wearing the colors too."

"She was?" Danielle smiled and shook her head.

"Yes. You need to see this girl. She is wearing bright red blouses, orange skirts, multicolored patterns, she's a trip. Gramps thinks there's another man in her life."

"You are kidding."

"No, I am not. Good-naturedly, he was going on about how he doesn't know what's come over her. Colors popping out all over. He said the guy must be an artist."

"Good for her. They are a kick, aren't they? We are so lucky Maria, aren't we? Gramps, Gram, Ma, Pa you couldn't pick a better generic stream then we got."

"You are right, Danielle."

"I mean that balance that you so positively portrayed, this discussion that we are having provides us with such a strong base of values and roles and relationships among people. The strength in our psychological, emotional, and interpersonal lives that we are given from our family is tremendous. If only all people walking the earth had a similar opportunity."

"I know, I think about it often when I see these children

from broken homes. They come to school and are very negative. They don't realize the value of learning. They never had the love we shared in our family."

"Ma and Pa provided us with so much. We talked about the spiritual dimension and did so much together. It wasn't only the exercising together, it was the consciousness of good health in all its dimensions, the good nutrition we learned at an early age. The mental dimension that was positively drilled in us to wonder, to push our intellect, to be lifelong learners."

"Yes, Danielle, and it was the joy, the play, the laughter, the valuing of differences of all peoples that was instilled in us at an early age. It was the positive reinforcement through Ma and Pa's friends from different ethnic backgrounds, even in Chicago-America's most segregated city."

"We also learned the value of community support. Understanding others, cooperating with everyone, regardless of who they were from every social strata and background. From Ma's caring nature and Pa's political and human expertise, we learned synergy among people. Those were human relations skills that everyone should be privileged to experience."

"As you were just articulating all those personal and family values, you know what I was thinking about?"

"No, what?"

"The financial lessons we learned as kids that kids today don't learn."

"You mean like earning a weekly allowance through assigned responsibilities at home?"

"Exactly."

"And learning to budget and save in order to go to the movie, purchase a new blouse, or have spending money when you go out with friends or on a vacation?"

"Yes. Kids aren't instilled with these concepts of earning, saving and investing money, or developing a budget for their present and future lives."

"Maria, you should try living in this town. For the first time we are dealing, truly dealing, with a budget and deficit. We are not talking hundreds or thousands or millions. We are talking about billions and trillions. It is ridiculous. Trillions of dollars and a deficit that is going to impact generations of people. Generations. And there's doubt about whether we can pass a crime bill this year to get guns off the street. Guns used by children that fire real bullets and kill people. Eighty to eighty-five percent of Americans want the guns off the street. Yet, year after year, the National Rifle Association beats the issue down in Congress. It's sick, sick, sick."

"Danielle, have you heard about the gang wars we are having in Chicago among ten to fourteen year olds. It is ridiculous. Where are the parents, the families, the communities, the politicians and why aren't they in a rage over this inhumane condition here in America?"

"Listen, Maria, you don't have to tell me. The New England Journal of Medicine had an excellent article talking about the public health hazard of guns. The United States Center for Disease Control has all kinds of statistics showing that if you have a gun in your home, the odds are higher someone close to you, in your family or among your friends, will be killed or injured by that gun. Do you think we care? Do you think we understand this logical and scientific thought? To what extent must we go to get the message across to people? It should be a front page story in every newspaper, every magazine, every radio, TV and movie until we get those guns off the street and out of the homes. It is insane! And, besides, America doesn't realize we are the most violent, supposedly civilized nation on earth."

"Danielle, Danielle, I agree with you. It is obvious that we have lived a very sheltered and parochial life to feel the way we do."

"Sheltered and parochial life, are you kidding? Pa was dealing with this issue decades ago, not to the extent that we and the legislatures are today. And Ma was helping to put lives together from bullets and knives and auto accidents for decades too. Maria, I beg to differ with you. We were not sheltered. Again, we were quite fortunate to understand through our parents' first-hand experience that bullets and guns maim and kill. It is as simple as that. And we need to do something significant in this country to reverse this madness. That's what it is, a madness that must be addressed. Be addressed to a greater level, an in-depth level, going to the sacredness of life and the sacredness of human beings, whether they are adults, or teenagers, or children. It is a disgusting situation in America and we must rise up and change it. We talk about health reform in this country. We don't know what we are talking about. We are talking about insurance reform. We are talking about tinkering with health insurance in this country. That's all. We need to talk about health in a broad sense. We need to talk about life insurance, again in the broad sense. We need to talk about the gut issues that you and I are discussing. We need to allow our children and teenagers to live in peace and abundance. And surely not regress to the Wild West, and to jungles, and to wars, where people are treated as poorly as animals, killing and maiming each other. We need to do something about it, and do it now."

"Danielle, when are you going to run for political office?"

"I don't know if ever. I do enough politics every day in this town. It has its frustrations. There is so much powerful parochial self-interest, that we don't know the serious issues from the political fluff. When young boys and girls are dying in Washington, Baltimore, Chicago, Boston, New York, Atlanta, Miami, Dallas, Los Angeles and San Francisco, it's time to do something serious to address unemployment, education and training, true health reform, racism, machismo, and every other issue that is a disease and a cancer. We get so wrapped up preserving the status quo rather than creating a rainbow of inclusion for all people. Women with equal pay for equal work. People of all colors sharing in the profits of Wall Street and Corporate America. It can happen. It will happen."

"Hallelujah!"

"Are you being funny or are you serious, Maria?"

"Of course I'm serious, serious delirious. I am your sister and your number one fan."

"Very funny."

"Where are you taking me to lunch, Danielle?"

"I'm going to take you to a little French restaurant in Great Falls, Virginia. You'll love it," said Danielle as she turned off the George Washington Parkway onto the Washington, D.C. Beltway.

"This place is exquisite, Danielle. I'll have to visit you more often," marveled Maria, as she looked out of the car window.

"You mean, here with a bright emotionally bent social activist female who loves an appreciative audience?"

"That's it, girl" said Maria.

* * *

"This way, ladies," said the charming and handsome

maitre d'. "How are you today, Danielle?" he remarked, with a pleasing look.

"Fine, thank you."

As he returned to the front of the restaurant, Maria inquisitively leaned toward her sister and stated, "He knows you, Danielle?"

"Yes, I have come here from time to time."

"From time to time. . . ."

"Yes, from time to time."

"With Robert or girlfriends?"

"Robert, girlfriends and others."

"Who are the others?"

"Others, what's the difference, people from the association, the association world, Washington, D.C. and friends."

"Male or female?"

"Yes usually."

"Very funny, Danielle. I'm serious. You can tell me."

"What do you mean, I can tell you?" Danielle remarked with a smirk on her face.

"I wanted to ask you about the corporate executive you almost had an affair with back in the eighties; have you come here with him?"

"I might have, why do you ask?"

"Have you come here recently with him?"

"No."

"Have you seen him recently?"

"No."

"Would you like to see him?"

"Maybe."

"When is the last time you saw him?"

"What is this, the witness stand or a nice restaurant for lunch?"

". . . or dinner?"

"Or dinner or whenever."

"Or whenever, that sounds interesting."

"What, are you on a reconnaissance mission for Ma and Pa or for yourself?"

"Just pursuing the essence of life as seen by the exciting and daunting Danielle."

"Well, you got it."

"So how's Robert?"

"He's fine. How's Anthony?"

"Anthony's great. You know how these Notre Dame attorneys are."

"I do?"

"Yes, remember when you dated Brian O'Quinn?"

"Boy, that's a name from the past."

"Brian's doing quite well. Heads a major firm with a lot of city contracts and contacts."

"He does, does he?"

"Yes. He asks about you from time to time."

"What does he ask?"

"How are you doing? What's happening in Washington, D.C.? Who are some of your contacts? You know, how these prima donna Catholic boys become as successful adults. They like to walk among the powerful. By the way, how is President Diane Jackson and Teddy?"

"President Diane is fine. Teddy is great too. They are both under attack constantly. But that comes with the territory."

"Do you think they are sorry they came, I mean with Theresa Phisler's suicide, the rumors surrounding that, and all the scandals involving Blackhawk, Kelly Bardin, Maria Smith, Haiti, Cuba and whatever else is breaking?"

"I don't think they are sorry they came. They are obviously learning every day, sometimes the hard way. The President has had tremendous successes. The Budget, social reform, international trade. But the pressure of the job is incredible. Some expectations can never be met, and she feeds into the multiplying expectations, trying to please everyone."

"She really is a crowd pleaser, isn't she?"

"With a dwindling support system."

"What do you mean?"

"Her father is dying. Her friends, Max Cable, Duke McMillian, etc. are having setbacks. People leave town or there is some changing of the guard. Change is the byline. And tonight's headlines drive the agenda."

"Danielle, what do you think of Lothrops Profile on the Jackson Administration that's just out?"

"For those of us in this town over several administrations, it is not that illuminating. Each president, each administration is different. They have different styles. Jackson likes to please; she always enjoyed being with the boys, different from being with the girls whom she also enjoyed. She loves lengthy discussions, exploring all sides of an issue, she wants to see the programs succeed, she'd like to see significant change but, politically, she fights pretty well for the incremental change. She and Teddy are very bright. It is just that this is Washington and it's quite a bit different than any other state capital, especially one as little as Raleigh, North Carolina."

"They went to Ivy League undergraduate schools."

"That's like saying Fred Ceberg is an experienced baseball commissioner. It may help but it is limited and there is nothing like Washington, D.C., with its history, traditions, players, and influences. Debbie Jefferson, who moved from the Office of Management and Budget to be her Chief of Staff, should help."

"What about Charkows, Firdley, Tarpel, Obduli and some of those closest to Jackson in the campaign?" inquired Maria.

"Oh, they may hang around and be helpful, but you'll see some shuffling of the players. Jackson wants to win. Every day. And whatever it takes, it takes. It is hard to understand her real values and priorities. Teddy is her salvation. She is very strong, even if beaten down this year by the press, especially as related to health reform. But don't kid yourself, these people have resiliency. As long as Teddy is there with her and their son Henry, she's okay. And she knows it."

"Danielle, can you imagine what they think of family and personal life?"

With a slight smile and some hesitation, Danielle remarked, "Yes."

"You do? What do you think it is in contrast with Ma and Pa?"

"Remember, both have interesting and somewhat different upbringings, even though they both went to Yale Law School. Her background was a bit problematic. Her father and grandparents raised her. His background was a little more traditional. Remember, his mother and father died this past year. Each has lost key role models in their lives. And then add Teresa Phisler's death."

"You mean suicide?"

"Yes, suicide!"

"Danielle, do you believe it was a suicide?"

"Yes."

"Do you think Teddy and his Chief of Staff had an affair sometime?"

"I don't know. It is possible. Anything is possible in the human condition."

"And especially with the President's spouse and his relationship with women."

"You know, Diane really is a remarkable person. I have been to the White House several times. I have seen her in different settings, different meetings. I have seen her with the high and mighty in the health and social welfare industry, as well as the low and weak. She is remarkable. She is a woman of compassion, and of purpose. Of strong convictions and values. Of empathy and understanding. She understands the health issues, all of them. Self-interests, like the health insurance industry, significant parts of the corporate sector, the small business sector, and other major health providers, have tremendous resources and are in this major complex political issue to the hilt. They have all been in this town for decades, have helped elect a lot of that Congress. Former Congressmen, like Phil Robertson, a Rhodes scholar, represent outside interests. But Diane is bright, articulate and learning all the time. She also tries to balance her personal interests with their professional ones."

"Excuse me, are you women ready to order?" their waiter asked.

"After our discussion I feel like I've had a full meal already," said Maria.

* * *

"Hi Robert."

"Hi, Maria, welcome to Washington."

They hugged.

"Danielle, how are you?" said Robert as he pecked her on the cheek. "So don't tell me, you had a great lunch, wonderful discussions and laughed much."

"How did you know?"

"Just a hunch. We well-trained cardiologists always go with the well played hunch or intuition if the scientific data is missing and a decision needs to be made."

"Guess where we went to lunch," continued Maria, as she attempted to gauge Danielle's and Robert's reactions.

"I don't have the faintest idea," he said.

"We went to Great Falls," said Danielle.

"Oh great."

"You've been there Robert?" inquired Maria.

"Of course, Danielle introduces me to all the fine things in life, including this area's best restaurants."

"Have you been there recently?" Maria solicited.

"I don't think so, why?"

"Oh I don't know, just wondered. The food was excellent. The setting exquisite."

"Sounds like when I was last there. When's dinner, honey?"

"Shortly."

"Great, I'm starved. Had a big day and just had a tuna sandwich around one o'clock."

"Well it will be just a few minutes."

"I'll change my clothes and be right back down," he remarked.

Maria turned to Danielle, "If you have children, you'll have to eat before eight, or you will have many meals without

Robert."

Lifting her left eyebrow, Danielle turned towards her sister Maria and said, "I know."

"So what's for dinner?" Robert asked as he entered the big kitchen.

"Lamb chops, caesar salad, mixed vegetables, your favorite home baked bread, and choice of wine," said Danielle.

"Excellent," returned Robert as they proceeded to sit down.

"So practice at the University was good, today?" Maria asked.

"Yes, exceptionally busy, some very interesting and challenging cases."

"Do you usually work this late?" Maria inquired.

"Sometimes it's later: it is usually a thirteen or fourteen hour day."

"Five or six days a week now?" Maria asked.

"Sometimes seven, but not all seven are thirteen or fourteen hour days."

"Goodness, what will you do when you have children, Robert?" Maria asked point blank.

Robert looked at Danielle. Danielle looked at Robert. Maria glanced at both.

"I guess we'll change our schedule then, won't we Danielle?"

Danielle nodded.

It was quiet for a moment or two. Then Maria continued on.

"How do you think you'll change your schedule, Robert?"

"Have you planned a baby for us soon?" Robert asked.

"Maria has two we can adopt," said Danielle. They all

29

laughed.

"So, Maria are you going to share one or two of your own or what do you think we ought to do?" asked Robert.

"I don't know, you seem pretty happy with your busy professional lives the way they are," said Maria.

"What are we missing?" inquired Robert.

"I don't know if you are missing anything. You are the only ones to determine that. We enjoy earlier dinners, around six o'clock with our two children. Then we both help them with homework. We watch very little television," said Maria.

"We watch very little television, unless I come home exceptionally early, like before 7 PM. Then I might catch the World News or I enjoy Political Talk with Mike Duncan and Shirley Shively. It is really lively. You see Danielle lives that kind of day everyday. This way I can be conversational with her."

Maria glanced at her sister, to see what her response would be, but there was nothing forthcoming.

"Danielle and I had a great conversation today, tracing our family life, which as you know was quite full and happy. We then talked about our current visions for our family and personal lives. We even talked about President Diane and Teddy."

"Of course," added Robert.

"Do you think Teresa Phisler's death was suicide?" asked Maria.

"The evidence seems to point that way," responded Robert.

"What about an affair between Teddy and Teresa?" asked Maria.

"I don't know, what do you think Maria?"

"I think they may have. Why else would such a brilliant

staff person, quite successful, go off and shoot herself in Washington? It seems like she could have returned to Raleigh to a successful career out of Washington. But it also seems like the issues and politics were coming quicker than she could assimilate, even for such a bright person. Throw in a personal relationship going back perhaps to Raleigh, as well as a close and longstanding professional relationship with Teddy, and who knows what might have happened. I'm sure you see situations in the hospital, where professional colleagues who work together long days and nights become personally entwined beyond the level that either initially thought feasible."

"I guess it is possible," said Robert.

Danielle chimed in, "Isn't the real issue larger? I think that President Diane and Teddy are an amazing story. For the first time we have a family in the White House that brings so much to a personal and professional relationship. These are very dedicated and committed people with tremendous skill and talent, who are trying to do the best they can to address America's domestic issues. Despite their vulnerabilities, or perhaps because of them, aren't their individual and family values the key to a better America? Have they taken the time individually and collectively to reevaluate and crystallize those visions for themselves first and then for America?"

"You are right Danielle," remarked Robert, "we don't take enough time, nor does the President and her spouse, to sort out our values. Who knows, after Maria leaves, we can do that."

"I'll leave early," contributed Maria.

The three of them laughed.

Danielle said, "Goethe, the German philosopher, said we have several roles as humans 'we must accept, give, relate to others, understand and feel our human existence.' I run into more people all the time who don't feel for themselves, much less for others. Who and what are we committed to? What is the individual meaning and purpose to our lives? Don't we realize that reflection on that fundamental thought is key to our potential as individuals and collectively as a community?"

"We surely don't cultivate our inner lives as much as we should," said Maria. "Danielle and I were remarking earlier today how lucky we were to have parents who were visionaries of their own individual lives as well as their family. Robert, you had great parents too, didn't you?"

"Yes. My father was an inspiration. He went to undergraduate school in Chicago at DePaul University, then Stanford Medical School where he became a great internist. My mother, like you Maria, was a teacher. She taught business education after graduating from the University of Indiana. There is a lot to say for those Midwest values."

"Robert, you have two brothers who have been quite successful professionally, as I recall," said Maria.

"Yes, one is an internist following in my father's footsteps. My younger brother is an attorney. My sister received a Ph.D. in anthropology at the University of Illinois."

"That's right, I forgot about her." said Maria.

"Not only are they successful professionally," remarked Robert, "I am also proud because of their personal contributions. Larry, the internist, and Paul, the attorney, both do pro bono work and participate in community projects like soup kitchens and Meals on Wheels. Stephanie is a Big Sister and does other volunteer work for young girls. She is a great mentor and role model."

"Wow, that's inspiring. Kahlil Gibran emphasized our responsibility to share our visions and inspirations. We are fortunate to recognize the value of each of us, especially when we take the time to find solitude and reflect on our lives as we should. As your brothers and sister have, Robert."

"Yes, we are fortunate to have been nurtured by those who love us. We need that love to dream the impossible dream and reach for the unreachable star. With a little hard work those visions can become real," said Robert.

"Yes, love and the flow of love in our life allows us to realize our values and our passions and to vision as family members, and as individuals, and to live happy, responsible and rewarding lives," remarked Danielle. "We must pursue our love, our love as a passion and our legacy. Ideally a legacy of passionate love."

Chapter 2
Be Responsible

A few weeks later, Robert and Danielle were having breakfast.

"I can't believe it's June already. Don't you just love summer?"

"I love everyday, whether it's summer, fall, winter or spring?"

"Oh, I know, but with summertime you know the season has switched. Spring and fall are like transitions. I still remember great summer times when we girls were kids. We would have picnics and be outside constantly. We'd look forward to and enjoy our vacation, usually near water and parks and nature, in Lake Geneva, Eagle River, or at the Michigan Shore. There was more freedom, it seemed. Freedom from school and from daily routine. And even now as adults it seems different. Summertime is concerts on the Capitol Lawn. Wolf Trap in Virginia. The Merriwether Post Pavilion in Columbia, Maryland. And there's baseball and the new Oriole's Park. Art fairs. With Pimlico's Preakness in May, the summer horse season was kicked off. There's polo. Trips to Annapolis and the ocean. Don't you know what I mean William?"

"William, did you say William?"

"I meant Robert. I was just reading about Supreme Court Justice William and how he recused himself from a case review because of a potential conflict of interest."

"Well, Cathryn."

"Okay, quit being funny Robert. I apologize. I offered an explanation. I'm sorry."

"Well, Danielle, yes, I do know what you mean. What

have you outlined specifically for us this summer? Surely we won't do all you outlined. I don't know exactly when I'll break away."

"I hope you'll be able to spare the first two weeks of August. I would like to make some concerts and art festivals this summer. And I would like to get to the ocean for a long weekend, at least if we plan to go to Colorado for those first two weeks of August."

"That seems reasonable and possible. We'll just need to plan it now. I have a very busy July, with the Health Maintenance Organization and Preferred Provider Organization negotiations. I know you're dealing with national health policy, but we are talking about some significant changes at the local level here in Washington, regarding reimbursement, cost shifts and accessibility. Some of these changes are incredible, real leaps of faith with unclear trade-offs."

"There are always trade-offs, Robert."

"I know there are trade-offs. But I am talking qualitative differences. It is like love. What are the trade-offs for love? We have a difficulty understanding what it is much the less what the trade-offs are."

"Robert, do you love me?"

"Well that's a crazy question. Yes, I love you. I have always loved you. And I always will. I am your most adamant admirer. Why do you ask? Especially after just calling me William."

"I told you I am sorry, Robert."

"I heard you Danielle. I just thought I would get your attention too."

"I guess I'm just wondering about love and its many facets. I was thinking about summer and the things we love to do together. I was thinking of the discussion last month when my sister Maria was here."

"Yes. Those were conversations. I think Maria loved being here. Sometimes I think she would like to live here. She seems to be fascinated by what you do and the political arena."

"But I was thinking about the first conversation we had. Remember you had gotten home about eight o'clock. And she was questioning you about having a baby and..."

"Do you want a baby?"

"Just a minute. Remember we were reminiscing about our parents and family and you were sharing with us about your folks, and brothers and sister..."

"Yes and?"

"And we were talking about what was real important to us. And what our values and priorities were."

"And..."

"And I am just reflecting on all that. I mean I want it all. For you. For me. For our family. And our friends. And for all those people who have little or nothing."

"That's why you are in the middle of this national health reform debate. You are the right woman. The right person in the right place."

"But I want to understand love in all its facets and live it."

"Well as far as I can see, you are understanding it and you are living it. Everyone should be as fortunate as you."

"You are lucky too, Robert. A leading cardiologist, and on a prestigious faculty, dealing with the most critical organ-the source of love."

"Danielle, what has gotten you so wound up this morning? You are on some kind of stream or flow, and I don't know where you are headed?"

"I don't know where I am headed either. I wish I knew."

"So do I."

"I just want to achieve my full human potential as an individual, and as your spouse. I want to vision the best for us and our families."

"That is laudatory. Maybe if we focus on one or two key attributes we can begin to perfect ourselves. But let's not forget our human fallibilities and limitations. I see people every day who have stretched their human limits. A heart has limits and nature must be respected."

"I know, Robert, I know. You see the physical evidence every day in your cardiology practice. What I am talking about is people being able to dream, to vision the utmost for themselves and their family. They need to stretch their spirituality, transcend their everydayness, stretch their emotions and their minds in positive ways. They need to look at each day and see its potential, at each individual they encounter and see that person's potential. That's how we will create a better earth."

"Danielle, I want to encourage you. I believe in you, I love you..."

"That's it Robert, we must start with love. That's what moves the world. Love is the idea I have been wrestling with along with others."

"Danielle, I don't want to interrupt you, especially as you are into something very important to both of us, but I had scheduled a golf game this morning and I really need to get moving, if I'm going to make it. Do you mind?"

"No, no, Robert, go ahead. I know how important that game is to you. I hope you shoot well."

"We can continue later this evening over dinner, if that is okay with you."

"Sure, sure, it will give me an opportunity to give all this more thought. And I can share all of it with you."

"Excellent," said Robert, as he kissed her on the cheek and went to get ready for his game.

Danielle began to clear the breakfast nook. It was a glorious day. June was another fabulous month in Washington, D.C. Usually not too hot. Oh, there might be some days in the nineties, but nights would be most reasonable. And there was always lots of sunshine. Danielle loved living in Chevy Chase. The tree-lined streets and unique houses were magical. The greens in the trees, bushes and grass blended with the morning sun. It was a storybook scene. Danielle loved their four bedroom house with library and finished basement. She had spent a lot of time finding the right finishing touches, the curtains, the knick-knacks, the wall hangings and pictures, every little detail one could imagine.

"See you later today," Robert yelled as he went out the front door.

"See you. Shoot well," Danielle yelled back.

Two hours later as Danielle cleaned, the phone rang. Danielle has been deep in serious thought regarding love, responsibility and other key concepts. She ran to get the phone in the master bedroom.

"Hello."

"Danielle."

"Barry, how are you?"

"I am fine. How are you?"

"Just, just wonderful."

"Great, I am glad to hear it."

Danielle's heart was racing.

"Danielle, I know this may be an inappropriate time to call, and I haven't given you much warning."

"No, no that's fine."

" Do you have time to have lunch today?"

"Well, let me think."

"Is Robert home today?"

"No."

After a few seconds elapsed, Danielle responded, "Yes, Barry, I'd love to have lunch with you."

"Great, how about 12:30 at the Potomac Landing in Alexandria Virginia?"

"Fine."

"I look forward to seeing you again, Danielle."

"I look forward to seeing you, Barry."

As Danielle hung up her phone, she could not believe she had heard from Barry. So quickly. They had made a lunch date to meet in a couple of hours. Danielle was elated and anxious. She wondered if she should have been so excited to hear Barry's voice and so willing to have lunch.

She thought of Robert, who she loved very much. But she also enjoyed Barry's company. It had been so long. Four or five years. She had seen him recently, testifying before Congress on health reform, as well as several times in the last year or two, in other health reform settings. There was the National Conference of State Legislatures (N.C.S.L.) annual meeting this past year in Denver.

Barry Mathews was a successful businessman from Tucson, Arizona. Danielle always thought he should run for Governor. Maybe he still might. He was only 42 years of age. Danielle had met him twelve years ago when she was 27. It was at the first N.C.S.L. meeting she had gone to, in San Diego. She would never forget it.

In Tucson, Barry had invested in real estate and the development of two resorts, the Loews Ventana Canyon and Westin's La Paloma at the base of North Mountain. Those two properties were among Danielle's favorites, with very good golf courses, excellent restaurants and beautiful desert surroundings.

My God, Danielle thought, what should I wear for lunch today? The last time she worried so much about her clothes was two weeks ago when she spent time with Senator William Hart from Virginia.

She was excited about seeing Barry, even though she believed that whatever attraction existed between them was over years ago. They had come to a mutual understanding. Both were happily married and neither was willing to leave their families or their spouses. They agreed they would always be friends. Not as close as they might have expected, given the explosive nature of their amorous relationship. Neither one had been willing to change, or make the sacrifices that were needed to make the relationship work.

But why now, after casually seeing each other these last few years, always in a professional setting, why were they now connecting again?

Danielle decided to wear the blouse and skirt with a jungle print to set off her long hair. Barry hadn't seen her in long hair. He would love it, Danielle mused to herself. She found some alluring old jewelry, including the snake shaped wristband that Barry had gotten for her ten years ago. She also wore the dainty gold necklace that Robert had purchased, as well as the green butterfly pendant that Senator Hart had recently given her.

Danielle could hardly wait to see Barry.

Barry, no doubt, could hardly wait to see Danielle.

Around noon, Danielle jumped into her Mercedes and

headed down Wisconsin Avenue toward Washington, D.C. She felt wonderful. The sun was shining brilliantly. It was about seventy-five degrees outside and there was a very soft breeze. Danielle had the top down. She played her Kenny G tape. The day had no parallel.

By this time she was in the heart of Washington, D.C. She passed by the White House and noticed women of many ages with signs protesting the abuse of women. For a second, Danielle thought she should be there with them, marching for the cause. Danielle was always moved by these fundamental causes for social justice and human rights. She often felt torn between being the activist and sacrificing of herself for others. She had found a niche in Washington, D.C., and within the health care associations trying to expand universal coverage for all people, especially women and children.

As Danielle crossed the 14th Street Bridge over the Potomac River and headed past National Airport and toward Alexandria, she shifted her thoughts to Barry. He was married with two children. That was one thing Barry had that Danielle didn't, she thought. The all-American family. A son and a daughter. Beautiful, brilliant young teenagers.

Danielle wondered what had moved Barry to call, especially on a Saturday morning at Danielle's house. Nevertheless, she was very excited to hear from him. Driving past the airport on George Washington Parkway and headed towards Alexandria, she realized she was going sixty-five miles an hour in a forty-five mile an hour zone so she quickly hit the brake. That is all I need, she thought, a speeding ticket. How would I explain that to Robert? Robert obviously doesn't know everything I do. What will I say if he asks me what I did today? I could say I had lunch with an old friend. And when he asks with whom, what do I say?

Do I even mention Barry and if so, how? Why don't I think about that after lunch? I will have hours before I see Robert. Or will I?

Danielle moved to the turning lane among the beautiful trees lining both sides of the Parkway. A natural grass and tree-lined mall divided the north and south routes of the Parkway. Danielle faced the entrance to the restaurant which also served as an entrance to the boats moored at the Potomac Landing as well as the park and picnic area to the right. As she proceeded towards the parking lot, she noticed a lot of activity among people working on their boats, getting ready to sail. Quite a contrast to weekdays when restaurant customers were in abundance and the boat users were few. Danielle found a parking spot on the left near the boats, a distance away from the restaurant. As she walked towards the restaurant, she began to wonder how Barry was getting to this restaurant. He hadn't mentioned where he was staying or coming from. Perhaps Danielle should have offered to pick him up. Was he in a cab or did he have a car and if so, what kind?

Danielle wondered if she was the first to arrive or whether he was waiting. It was about twelve twenty-eight. She walked into the restaurant and glanced around. She didn't see him.

"Hello, Danielle, how are you today?" said the hostess.

"Hello, Amy, fine and you?"

"What brings you here on a Saturday? I don't know that I've ever seen you here on the weekend."

"Oh, an old friend called and asked me to lunch."

"No one has asked for you yet. Is it a man or woman?"

"A man."

"Danielle."

Danielle quickly turned and saw Barry. "Barry, How are you? So good to see you," she said as they warmly embraced each other with eyes closed. Barry was a handsome man. Six foot two, around one hundred and ninety five pounds, with a body like Joe Montana or Joe Namath. He was much better looking than those jocks. He looked like Clark Gable. Dark hair, a black mustache, deep penetrating eyes. He hugged - like your father would have after graduating from college.

"Danielle. You look great. Smashing. It's good to be with you. I am so glad you were able to make lunch."

The hostess intervened, "Can I show you to your table by the water."

Barry stepped back and said, "After you Danielle."

As Danielle walked, she could again feel her heart pounding. She felt like she was floating, as she approached the table for two near the water in the corner of the restaurant.

"Where would you like to sit, Barry?"

"On a chair near the window and you? Which chair do you wish to sit in, Danielle?"

"I don't care, but if you insist I will take this one," Danielle remarked as she took the one with a view of the water. Barry's seat faced the back wall, but he didn't care because he was completely focused on Danielle.

"Well, what brings you to Washington, D.C. on a Saturday in June?" asked Danielle.

"You," said Barry.

"Really?" asked Danielle. She knew there was more to his visit than just herself.

"Actually I was in New York the last couple of days and just flew in this morning."

"Why didn't you tell me? I could have picked you up at the airport."

"I thought I might be delayed, and didn't want to make you wait."

"It would not have been too much," said Danielle, imagining how they might have hugged more romantically at the airport, although she probably would have been seen by Robert's and her friends in National Airport. "What was in New York?" She asked.

"I am expanding some real estate development in Arizona and Colorado and needed to see some financial people regarding a potential joint venture."

"That makes sense."

"Yes, I am quite excited about it. You know the success I've had in Tucson and the surrounding area. Colorado is undergoing a boom. Some reports indicate that it is the largest state in the United States undergoing significant economic development. Idaho and Montana along with Utah and Nevada are also growing. The West is where it's at."

"I know, Barry, we've talked about that in the past. But Washington is still the most exciting place to be."

"That's why I am back here. So how are things going for you with health reform?"

"Exciting, challenging, you know we talked briefly in February when we saw each other on the Hill. Remember the Congressional testimony you gave and the discussion we had in the Dirksen Building?"

"How could I forget it," Barry responded, looking longingly into Danielle's gorgeous eyes. She returned the favor.

"So why are you really here in Washington, though I am flattered you called?" said Danielle.

"Well, as you know there's more House Ways and Means Health Subcommittee hearings beginning on Monday, and I will testify again on Tuesday."

Danielle hesitated, wondering to herself why he didn't

come in Sunday night. She decided to ask him directly. "Why didn't you stay in New York and come down Sunday night?"

"Because I like Washington better than New York. I thought I might be able to see you. And even if I didn't, there were other options down here."

Danielle wondered what or who those options might be. Yet, despite her concern, she was glad Barry had reached her at home, before catching the eleven o'clock air shuttle from New York to Washington, D.C.

"Well, thanks for the call this morning and this invitation to lunch."

"My pleasure," Barry responded.

"Our pleasure," Danielle boldly stated. By his eyes Barry agreed.

"You know, that's what's great about our relationship, Danielle. We can pick up at any time, any place."

"That's true, to an extent."

"To an extent?" Barry inquired.

"You know what I mean, Barry."

"Do you really feel that way, Danielle?" Barry tested her.

"Yes, I love you very much, as you love me very much, but I also love Robert, and you love Julie."

"But we'll always have something special between us."

"Yes, but that was years ago." They had shared a close relationship for seven years, after meeting at an N.C.S.L. meeting. Danielle had just started with the American Medical Association in their Washington, D.C. office as a lobbyist for federal or national issues. Prior to that she had been with the Assistant Secretary of Health working in government relations and health issues involving the Department of Health and Human Services as well as the White House and Congress. She was greatly committed to her job and her cause. When their relationship cooled a handful of years ago, Danielle was positioned as Executive Director for the Women's Health Caucus, a national alliance of women's and children's groups concerned with better health and related issues. At that time Danielle had probably initiated and felt most strongly about modifying their close seven year relationship.

"Well, Danielle, how about some wine to start our lunch?"

"A White Zinfandel, please."

"Make it a bottle of your best, if you will," said Barry. He pointed to the wine list and turned to the waitress, who had been listening and waiting patiently.

"Danielle, we have always shared much. We met professionally, yet connected and communicated personally on many levels," said Barry.

"I don't wish to return and expand all these levels Barry, although you might like to."

"Give our friendship a chance, Danielle."

They laughed.

"You haven't changed, Barry, have you? Always trying to stretch a good thing. Pushing our friendship to its limits."

"What else deserves so much of our energy?"

Danielle was stumped. A bit startled for the moment. It didn't happen often to Danielle. Usually she was the one with quick fresh comments, pointed questions or cut through statements. But this time, she reflected on Barry's comment. That's what she loved about Barry. He could be so deep. She knew Barry well, and he was deep. He was serious and intense, but also had a great sense of humor.

At that moment, the wine came and Barry offered a toast. "To our unwavering friendship and love, our search for meaning, individually and together, and to this beautiful lunch in Washington. May we have many more."

She tapped her glass against his, and as she did, wondered whether she should counter his toast with one of her own. But like a good politician, she held her tongue, and sipped her wine.

"So, many more lunches?" she teased him.

"Why not, unless you insist on dinners."

"Or breakfast."

"Or just a drink," he gamely responded.

"Barry, how would you describe love?"

"You mean between us?"

"Between us and friends like us, but also in a broader sense. Like the love between you and Julie or me and Robert." Danielle had the ability to get to the heart of the matter.

"Great question, Danielle. I have been thinking about it for a long time. For the past twelve years with you. Those first seven years where we shared so much. And those last handful of years where we have shared interesting exchanges as well as brief glances. Love to me means nurturing, being compassionate, helping one another, sharing. What does it mean to you, Danielle?"

"Similar things, but also being responsible, nurturing responsibility, being compassionately responsible, helping each other responsibly, serving responsibly, and sharing responsibly."

"That's an interesting and appropriate twist. We've often discussed what was responsible love between us," Barry said.

"That's why we stopped seeing each other. We loved each other so intensely, yet perhaps not as responsibly as we should have," said Danielle.

"If you really believe that, why did you agree so readily to this lunch?" asked Barry.

"Because we could always have a great lunch. And I was ready for lunch on this beautiful June Saturday."

"Lunch with me or lunch with anyone?" Barry inquired.

"Maybe lunch with anyone, but this is lovely with you," said Danielle, glancing at him playfully. They always had a good time with each other. But, it was unclear whether what they shared was just a game, a friendship or true, responsible love.

Danielle knew on this day it was for real. Both were enjoying the presence of each other. The circumstances couldn't be more beautiful. Why didn't she and Robert feel exactly like she was feeling now with Barry? Maybe they did, but she took Robert for granted.

"I think love and responsibility may be linked, but to be fully appreciated, they need to be considered as separate attributes, to be fully understood and realized in all their magnitude," Barry offered.

"I agree," responded Danielle. "Tell me more."

"Love and responsibility are two of the richest words. Love and responsibility give meaning to our lives in all of their aspects. It is like the love and responsibility we feel towards each other, as well as our spouses and our families, our professional colleagues and friends," Barry commented before being interrupted by Danielle.

"And those less fortunate who really need our love and our sense of responsibility for their welfare," she strikingly added.

"...and to those less fortunate who really need our love and our sense of responsibility for their welfare," Barry reiterated word for word, as he was talented enough to do. "That's one of the things I love about you, Danielle. It is your sensitivity and compassion for those less fortunate. You will never lose that nineteen sixties' edge regarding social activism even if you are 39 and not in your fifties."

She glanced at him over her wine. "Thanks very much for the compliment, but compassion for and service to others has no age limit," Danielle responded.

"By the way, how does it feel to be almost 40?" Barry asked.

"It's great," Danielle responded without missing a beat. "Unlike you I'm less than halfway home, maybe only thirty-three to forty percent, seeing that I plan on living to one hundred and twenty years of age."

"Halfway home, am I? I think I might live beyond eighty-four years of age, thank you."

"But the pace at which you live, Barry. It would have most men dead well before eighty years of age. How much of the time are you traveling or away from home?"

"Away from Tucson?"

"Yes."

"About fifty to sixty percent of the time, I guess. I've got some development going on near Phoenix, in Scottsdale and also near Flagstaff toward the Grand Canyon. Plus I do this traveling east, primarily Washington, D.C., New York and some travel to Boston and Atlanta. Why do you ask?"

"If you really loved your wife and child, would you be gone most of the time?"

Barry hesitated. Not like him. "Are you trying to make me feel guilty?" asked Barry.

"No, not at all. You and I have talked before about the value of guilt. Unlike many others, we don't appreciate the positive value of guilt. That's not to say we have no soul, but we like to focus on more positive emotions."

"Then why did you say what you did, Danielle?"

"Maybe because I think you ought to reflect on the value of love, love for yourself, your spouse and your children."

"I do."

"So what's your answer to my question?"

"I can love them all with less than fifty percent of my time, so I can accumulate more wealth and riches for them long term, and help others to develop real estate, buy homes, start businesses and do other things that provide people the opportunity to show love in many ways. How is that for an answer?" Barry took a sip of water and looked into Danielle's eyes-without blinking.

"Fine, if you truly believe it and think that's a responsible answer, then it shows responsible love."

"And how about you, Danielle?"

"What do you mean?"

"How much time do you spend with Robert and how do you feel about your time spent with those you love?"

"I spend as much time as possible with Robert. He's a successful cardiologist and puts in long dedicated hours, but he makes sure we have quality time together."

"Is it the optimum quality time possible?" inquired Barry.

Danielle hesitated before responding. "I suppose we could spend more and better time together, if we thought about it and modified our schedule somewhat."

"Is it like our time together now?" Barry reached out for her hand. She grasped his right hand tightly and emotionally.

"Sometimes it is," she quietly offered as she sensed Barry's warmth. For a moment she was at peace. She reflected on it and enjoyed it, then slowly withdrew her hand and felt it begin to cool down.

"Thank you for your hand, Danielle."

"You are welcome, Barry." They looked into each other's

eyes without smiling.

"Barry I appreciate being with you. Sipping our wine, holding hands together. But I am serious about knowing what love is in all its depth. And I want to know what responsibility and accountability mean in all their dimensions. And what responsible love means in each and every circumstance that one can identify."

"We've always shared those thoughts with each other Danielle."

"I know. But what if our relationship was on the front page of the Washington Post and the Tucson Daily? How then would we feel? How would you feel then?"

"I guess I would feel those were the risks I took for love. And I would still love you very much."

"But what about Julie and your two children? How would they feel? Wouldn't they be hurt?"

"Maybe. Probably. But that doesn't mean I don't treasure my love and respect for you."

"Love, respect, and responsibility?"

"Yes, responsibility too."

"How can you say that Barry? Are you being thoughtful? Are those the reasonable reflections of a disciplined man? Is that showing stewardship for me, your wife, and your two children? Is that the kind of example and mastery of yourself and responsibility for the situation you want to communicate to them and others?" Danielle asked.

"Well, obviously as you articulated, that's a tall order and I am a limited and fallible human person," Barry exclaimed.

"A limited and fallible human being? You are a strong and successful businessman, a model spouse and father in the eyes of many. I know you Barry, and I love you, but I have been thinking and thinking about what I am sharing with you. I recognize the limits of our love and our relationship. I feel constrained by those limits, while at the same time I want to honor them."

"Danielle, I love you. That is what I know. I am willing to clean up whatever mess I make, as Robert Fulghum wrote many years ago in his book about everything he learned in kindergarten."

" I just reread that book in the last couple of months."

"You did?"

"Yes. I have been reading everything that relates to the fundamental principles and values in our lives. You know, like Covey's <u>Seven Principles</u> and Bennett's <u>Book of Virtues</u>."

"Like everyone else I bought Covey's book. I heard him speak years ago, before he was famous. He gave a very passionate presentation. When I heard him again years later, he wasn't as passionate, but his message was still most meaningful."

"Maybe he was tired," Danielle commented.

"Yes, it could have been burnout. He said he wasn't going to do as many public speaking engagements. He was going to do more by video, and spend more time on reflection."

"Everyone should do more reflection," Danielle stated. "In this town especially. I am convinced Congress, other parts of the federal enterprise and all of the self interests should shut down for three to six solid months each year to read, reflect and share meaningful dialogue. That would be more productive than meaningless Congressional hearings, heated discussions and blaming one another. There isn't enough communication between the public and private sectors, between one agency and another, and between the executive branch and Congress. There is far too little discussed meaningfully with the judicial branch, whether it is the Supreme Court or other judicial entities. Our justice system is not functioning optimally. It will be interesting to see what the November elections bring. I remember previous elections when Americans were frustrated with Congress and yet very few incumbents lost."

"Danielle, it just represents the cynicism and apathy that sometimes exists in this country when things are too comfortable, and we haven't had a major crisis. The same is true of the corporate sector and of government at the state and local levels. Until it gets to crisis proportions or unless there is significant trauma, the American people and their thick skins and set ways aren't penetrated. Ask the common everyday Joe on the street about love, responsibility, respect for life and other deep issues. At first they are taken back that you asked the question. Then they are moved positively if some skilled facilitator is able to make them spend time reflecting on what is really important in their lives."

"Barry, do you think about this as much as I do?"

"Probably not. But I do reflect on it. And like you I try to do better every day in a conscious positive way. That's why I called you."

"Thank you, Barry."

They ordered lunch and their meals came. Danielle had lamb chops, Barry the salmon. It had been years since they had eaten a meal together. Their discussion was as rich as it had ever been, perhaps richer, given their increased maturity and wisdom. When they first met, they were younger and more willing to take risks, stretch the limits of love.

Expanding on his prior comment Barry said, "Maybe we try to be more positive because of the Christian Coalition and its emphasis on family values, before Rush Limbaugh came on to the scene. Isn't he tough to stomach? Has America deteriorated so much to allow such a negative entertainer to take front stage? Who are the good and respected leaders of our time? Surely not the avalanche of talk show hosts like Gordon Liddy, Don Imus and Howard Stern. Perhaps some of those guests on Larry King, Charlie Rose, Oprah Winfrey and C Span with Brian Lamb will become our new leaders."

"I would agree," said Danielle.

They continued to discuss those and other issues of the day, as well as their memories together. Dessert was a treat. Danielle had an extremely rich devil's food cake that melted like chocolate mousse. He ordered french vanilla ice cream with raspberries, strawberries and kiwi. They both loved it.

It was now time to depart. Or was it? It was three fifteen.

"Well, Barry, thank you. I really enjoyed the lunch and the company." She cautiously smiled and looked directly into his deep brown eyes.

"I will always enjoy being with you."

There he goes again, stretching the good times into the realm of the unknown, she thought. "Have you paid the bill?" she inquired.

"Yes."

She moved first to get up. She was ambivalent and wondered if he would have ever moved had she not gotten out of her seat.

"Thank you again, Barry," she said.

"Thank you," he smiled.

They made their way to the door. Outside, the sun was still high in the west, but not as high as when they had each entered the restaurant.

"Do you need a ride somewhere, Barry?" Danielle turned toward him.

"Yes, the Loews L'Enfant Plaza, that Associated Luxury Hotel."

"What a lovely place," Danielle said as she reflected on previous visits to that hotel. It had a wonderful location and ambiance. "Will you head back home Tuesday or Wednesday?" Danielle innocently inquired.

"Tuesday night after testifying and making some Congressional visits."

They got in her convertible, with the top down, and cruised down the George Washington Parkway, across the 14th Street Bridge, towards Washington. To the left, the Lincoln Memorial, the Jefferson Memorial and the Washington Monument stood in all their splendor on this beautiful June day. Danielle and Barry were quiet during the short drive to downtown Washington. Occasionally they glanced at each other and smiled.

As they were about to turn towards the Loews L'Enfant Plaza hotel Danielle said, "The President is in, if you would like to see her this weekend or before you leave Tuesday."

"I am sure she and Teddy have more important people to see."

"Than moi and vous?"

"Yes."

"Well, here we are," said Danielle, pulling into the Loews L'Enfant driveway.

"So we are," said Barry as he reached for his small black leather bag. "Would you care for an after lunch drink or another dessert?"

As much as she was tempted, Danielle coolly and without missing a beat said, "I'll take a rain check or a sunshine check, if I may."

Hesitating, Barry said, "You may." He leaned over to kiss

her on the cheek. She leaned towards him. They kissed, eyes closed, lips connected. Danielle was first to separate.

"Thanks again, Barry, it was great to see you."

"Great to see you too," he smiled and stood back, looking longingly at her.

"Have a great stay. Maybe I'll see you at the hearing on Tuesday."

"Do you want to make plans to get together?"

"No. I have a busy week, especially Monday and Tuesday."

"Well, you know where I am if you change your mind."

"Thanks again Barry. For everything."

They blew each other another kiss as she pulled out of the driveway. On the drive home, she reflected on what responsibility meant in her relationship to Robert, in her relationship to Barry, and in her relationship to Senator William Hart.

Chapter 3
Be Truthful

The summer had already been hot and it wasn't even July fourth. Danielle had been busy this past month with several Congressional subcommittee hearings on health reform. She had spent a substantial time visiting the appropriate congressional leaders regarding the issue. It was going to be a tough fight. Health reform was a complex issue, and the multitude of interests wanting to have their say seemed to multiply. There were health insurance and corporate interests, the small business concerns, along with doctors, hospitals and other health professions. The American Hospital Association, the American Medical Association, the Federation of Health Systems and the American Nursing Home Association were quite active. Even the health groups representing providers and consumers preferring the home setting, like the American Association of Home Care and the National Association of Home Care, were active. Fighting for equal time were the consumer interests from such groups as the American Association of Retired Persons, Families USA, various retired union interests, and Medicare constituencies, the National Council of Senior Citizens, the Seniors Council and various women's groups, black and Hispanic caucus groups, children's groups like the Children's Defense Fund, Juvenile Diabetes, various charitable groups like the American Heart Association, American Cancer Society, American Diabetes Association, etc.

Other voices also joined the debate. The more traditional and diverse provider groups like the American Academy of Family Physicians, American Academy of Pediatrics, American College of Surgeons, American College of Physicians and American

Society of Internal Medicine were now joined by subspecialty groups like the American College of Cardiology, American Academy of Orthopedic Surgeons, American College of Emergency Physicians and other agencies and coalitions cutting across these and other medical groups, like group practices, health maintenance organizations and preferred provider groups. And then there was the American Nurses Association with its million plus constituents, the multiple specialty organizations of nurses, occupational therapists, physical therapists, psychologists, respiratory therapists, speech pathologists and various other therapist groups and health professions vying for attention. Danielle wasn't surprised that little progress in health care reform was forthcoming despite the proclamations of Presidents and Presidential candidates. Historically, the ones who lacked appropriate resources were the people who really needed help.

In the early years of the debate, the American public seemed to be behind the President. It seemed possible that Congress would respond with much more than single health insurance tinkering. It seemed like they would assure that someone could not be excluded from health insurance because of a pre-condition, and that people could take their insurance from one job to another. And maybe there would be some medical malpractice reform so doctors wouldn't have to leave practice and there would be added preventive care insurance coverage and maybe some basic, yet limited long term care for the American public.

But as the year progressed, it began to look tougher for any health reform legislation. Both parties turned it into hot air debates by Presidential candidates. Danielle thought the best opportunity for the Jackson Administration and the Democratically controlled House was in the President's first year or early second year while the President still had the support of the American public. Once the well-financed Health Insurance Association of America had their successful Harry and Louise ads rolling before the American public, and the corporate sector and small business interests including the small business administration started hammering away at the employee's mandate part of the Jackson plan, there was increasing concern raised with true health reform. Together with the continuing powerful tobacco interests who limited the amount of tax that was going to be added, there were minimal dollars being found to finance the needed health reform. Costs in the health industry began to be modified, and that was publicized. So cost increases shrank from the nationwide concern a year prior.

Recognizing the difficult state of affairs regarding health reform, Danielle was not depressed, but more resolute as she went to meet her close friend Senator William Hart, Democrat from Virginia. Senator Hart was a newer member of the Senate Finance Committee and its Subcommittee on Health. He had served for six years on Senator Harrigan's Labor and Education Committee's Subcommittee on Health. That committee was always more sensitive to the pressing needs of the American public's health and welfare. Historically known as a liberal authorizing committee of the Senate, the Subcommittee's positions were usually modified considerably by the influence of the more conservative committees of the Senate, like Finance and Budget, before a bill went forward. Senator Hart had been pushing for years to get on to the more powerful Senate Finance Committee and had succeeded in the past two years.

Senator Hart was to meet Danielle at the Hawk and Dove Restaurant at noon this July 4, following a morning rally on the Capitol steps by several veterans groups. It was just up from the

Capitol on Pennsylvania Ave. It was already a half hour after noon, and Senator Hart wasn't there. Danielle decided to go and wait outside in the gorgeous sunny and eighty-five degree day.

Within ten minutes, Danielle spotted the Senator coming towards her, with the beautiful Capitol and shiny white buildings, including the Library of Congress, in the background.

"Good afternoon, Danielle, sorry I am late," said Senator Hart.

"That's understandable, Senator. When constituencies demand your time, especially veterans on the Fourth of July, you must respond."

"Well, thank you for your understanding," he said as they quickly but warmly embraced. "I was surprised you would be in town on the fourth," said the Senator.

"Well, Robert and I discussed it. He really needed to practice on Saturday. I had warned him that I might be tied up part of today. Robert and I had an enjoyable Sunday in Annapolis," she volunteered.

"You and I need to return to Annapolis or St. Michael's again," the Senator responded. "It was extremely healing for me."

Danielle hesitated as they entered the restaurant. "Yes that would be enjoyable."

They proceeded to a corner table, as much out of the traffic flow as possible. The restaurant wasn't very crowded.

"I am surprised the restaurant is open," the Senator said.

"Well, with the tourists in this long weekend, I guess they thought there might be more business," Danielle offered.

"Well, Danielle, it is great to see you," the Senator smiled.

"I always enjoy my time with you, Senator."

"Danielle, this is hard, isn't it. Stealing an hour together here and there. Does it bother you as much as it bothers me?"

"William," she said. "I think we do pretty well. And it is more complex than just two people finding time for each other." "I know, Danielle. I know. It is just that we are both wrestling with being truthful and honest and sincere with ourselves and our loved ones."

"William, believe me, I wrestle with it too. My graduate work and professional experience teaches me about fundamental ethical values. I try to live by those principles, but my weaknesses and human limitations sometimes get the better of me."

"I know what you mean."

"I have spent several years reading and analyzing the writings of best selling authors, international leaders, and other inspirational thinkers who address their fundamental ethical values and principles," Danielle said.

"I know, we've talked about Covey, Bennett, Russ Kidder's Shared Visions and James Liebig's Merchants of Vision."

"Yes and Scott Peck's Road Less Traveled and Thomas Moore's Care of the Soul. I understand black lies and white lies. I have and continue to reflect on learning what it means to be authentic, and to be real, to have integrity. I intellectually have considered what truthfulness really is, and I believe we must continue to learn, to search for the truth in all things." Danielle shifted slightly in her seat. "Living that truth is more challenging."

"Why are you sharing this with me?"

"I am not sure I fully know. Yes, Robert and I could have had a long weekend together this weekend. But you have been so busy lately, I wanted to see you today."

"And I wanted to see you."

"William, I do not want to end our relationship. I only

61

want to ask where it is headed?"

William was silent, yet focused on Danielle. He began to reflect on how much he enjoyed her company. Her directness. Her honesty. Her integrity. He loved to look at her, be with her, and talk with her.

"Danielle, I love you very much. I don't know where it is headed. Those of us in the national political spotlight, as you well know, don't ever know what the next headline is going to read, much less anticipate all the stories behind the headlines. I enjoy the present. The present within the context of the historical past and in joyful and optimistic anticipation of the future. I am fueled by our deep relationship and for that I am grateful, Danielle," William looked empathetically and lovingly at her.

She stared longingly into his gorgeous eyes, feeling all of him. At fifty-five years of age, he looked forty-five or younger. An athletic six foot one inch with a body like a young marine, William was very distinguished with that blond, dishwater brown hair and young Paul Newman look. At times he displayed the youthfulness of Steve McQueen. He had a great sense of humor, yet he was as deep and as serious about his role as a United States Senator as anyone could be. William loved to challenge the establishment. He wanted a new and better order for all people. He had come from relatively modest means. His father was a small farmer in Charlottesville. His mother had been a school principal. Like Danielle's parents, William's family had been politically active in Charlottesville and in the State of Virginia. It was when William went to Harvard Law School and when he returned to Washington to clerk at the Supreme Court that he had become more cognizant of the national and international dimensions of politics. In fact, he had served at the State Department's General Counsel's office and had also received a master's degree in international relations at Georgetown University. He had later returned to Charlottesville to open a successful law practice, later teaching at the University of Virginia law school. He served two terms in the United States House of Representatives before entering the Senate at age forty-seven. Now two years into his second term, he was experienced, he was respected and he was feeling his power and influence.

After what seemed like an eternity of silence, the Senator continued, "Danielle, what are you thinking, what are you feeling?"

"I am feeling good," she responded. "I am feeling fortunate, fulfilled, confused, torn, yet emotionally moved. It is like Mihaly Csikszentmihalyi says in his book, <u>Flow</u>, I am in the flow. I am whitewater rafting. It is a hell of a ride, exhilarating. It is rough in spots, but it is a very fast current that one searches for on the river or on the roller coaster, at the amusement park. I love it, despite the risk, despite the danger, despite any negative consequences."

"That's a great description," William commented. "I feel like I am there with you."

"You are, William, you are. It is just that every whitewater raft ride comes to an end, as we come to solid earth again to regain our stability and natural order."

"Danielle you commented earlier regarding truthfulness, sincerity, integrity. What about the element of fairness? Have you thought much about what fairness means today?"

"I have as a matter of fact. It is very much related to responsibility. Yet it is distinct. And many authors have described difficult aspects of fairness. It is a concept that is coming more into its own in America and in the world. With our civil rights history and our attempts for inclusion in this country, the concept of fairness will continue to flourish. Fairness and inclusion are two reasons Jackson was elected President and why she may be re-elected, if there is not some significant economic or international upheaval. In America, we emphasize a win/win philosophy. This philosophy is an integral part of our negotiations, our sports traditions and our politics. In all three of these arenas, winning is everything. But win/win is not an accurate philosophy." said Danielle.

"What do you mean?"

"It is just not all- encompassing and true, William. Let me explain," said Danielle. "When you won your election, how was that a win/win for your opponent?"

"Well, that's different," the Senator returned.

"But let's look at any issue. Do you really believe both parties win evenly, fairly?"

"Well, no, you are right."

"You have been in numerous negotiations. In politics, in legal matters, in a variety of business matters. Though people may have normally subscribed to a win/win philosophy, did the different parties, in fact, both win, evenly and fairly?"

"No, probably not."

"Of course not."

"Then, what are you proposing in its place?"

"A win/learn philosophy," she exclaimed.

"Win/learn, what is that? If you don't win, you learn, so maybe you can win next time based on what you learned?"

"Exactly. If you are a lifelong learner, you always learn. And if you win at something, be it love, a game, or a business deal, so be it. If you lose, and you have the perspective of a lifelong learner, you learn something, rather than lose. And learners are winners. Whether it is the President in her book, explicitly emphasizing the concept of America being a nation of lifelong learners, or it is educational experts or psychologists and philosophers calling for lifelong learning, a win/learn philosophy will allow us to make more progress in this country than ever before."

"Do you have a piece of legislation, Danielle, that I can introduce?"

"Are you making fun of my serious philosophy?"

"Not at all. I am serious."

"If we had legislation that might kill the concept."

"Very funny. You are the one being facetious now."

"I am not," said Danielle. "I couldn't be more serious."

"I think you are on to something. I think the win/learn concept is a good one and needs to be developed."

"I have been developing it for years. It is a philosophy I have subscribed to for a long time. It is the essence of my professional and personal survival and success."

"Survival and success," said William amused. "I have survived and felt I would always survive, despite any setback, political or otherwise. Many of us, because of our parents and our environment have been given much, including the opportunity to thrive. Not all are as privileged. An emphasis on learning in this country, especially with all the change going on will propel us to be even more successful, understanding and fair, and to truly pursue life, liberty and happiness."

"Exactly," Danielle concurred. "Lifelong learning needs to be our credo. Not win/win, that is a philosophy espoused by the elite and those in control to make everyone think they are winning on the more dominant party's terms."

"So you have concluded that this win/learn philosophy will be more fair and truthful?" asked William.

"Yes. A win/learn philosophy is more true, more real to life than win/win where one party usually wins more than the other party. Win/learn is a true paradigm shift. A win/learn philosophy encourages us to learn, and to then apply that knowledge. It will enhance social equity among all peoples. People will be rewarded for their effort to learn, to contribute to new and better learning, to the development of new knowledge bases. It ties right into our internet and e-commerce culture. A win/learn philosophy will build a loyalty and commitment for all of us to be more loyal to one another. We will be as concerned about the ending of relationships and deals as we will the beginning and existence of relationships. Thomas Moore, in Care of the Soul, raised our sensitivity and consciousness regarding this critical perspective of the endings of relationships. We must take greater care of one another," said Danielle.

"How can you and I take greater care of one another?" asked William.

Danielle was taken back. She was on one of her intellectual trips. Her mind was going two-forty. She was conceptually developing the philosophies of love and win/learn in grand terms. Now William had turned the question and her words towards her and their relationship.

"What do you mean, William?" asked Danielle stalling for time to think.

"I mean how can we care more for each other? How can I care for you?"

Danielle was really moved by William. She knew that what they shared was more profound than what she shared with Barry and Robert. Or was it? Robert had been the most loving person she had known, until she met William.

"I don't know, this lunch with you is beautiful. Being

here, talking, sharing our thoughts, drinking White Zinfandel together. It is all very beautiful," she replied. But she wasn't responding to his question, and she didn't know how to respond. Her heart was beating rapidly.

Although Danielle had heard about William when he first came to the Senate, she did not really know him well until two years ago, when he was running for re-election and his wife of 27 years died of cancer during the campaign. Her death had hit him hard. He and his wife had a very good family and personal life with two wonderful grown daughters, now twenty-three and twenty-five years old. The oldest daughter married a professor at the University of Richmond and she herself was a local television personality in Richmond. William's youngest daughter was in law school at the University of Virginia.

Danielle found herself reminiscing about her first memorable contacts with William during that campaign and how their relationship had evolved since that time. Both had been involved at various levels in the election of the President. She and William had shared much over those past two years philosophically, politically, intellectually, and intimately. She was in a personal dilemma of the deepest dimensions. She loved her husband, but she also loved William.

"Danielle, Danielle, do you hear me?" asked William, breaking her concentration.

"Yes. Yes, of course. I was just reflecting on your questions. I don't know how you can care for me more." But she could. She just couldn't get herself to say it now. As she regained a sense of herself, she turned the question to him, "How can I care more for you?"

"How do you want to care more for me, Danielle?"

She sank into her chair, into herself. "How do you want

me to care more for you, William?"

Now there was silence between them.

"I don't know," William responded.

Danielle was feeling a bit stronger. "William, we should be more open with each other about this subject. Don't you agree?"

"Yes."

"Okay, let's each consider how we can care for each other, either individually, or collectively."

"Okay. Do you want to start?"

"Whoever," she said.

"Okay, I'll start. It might be easier for me because my wife is dead."

Right, thought Danielle. She was in a bigger personal dilemma than William.

"Danielle. I love you very much. I love you more than any woman I know. I loved my wife. But she has been dead two years. And you are refreshing, stimulating and loving. You and I have shared much professionally and politically the past two years. You have shared yourself fully with me these past two years as fully as any woman can express herself. And I appreciate that. I repeat. I love you very much. I know you have a loving relationship with Robert. As a cardiologist, he truly understands the heart. And I don't wish to do anything to harm you, Robert, or your relationship. I have too much respect for you."

"And I greatly respect you, William, as a person, as a United States Senator, as a father," added Danielle.

"Well then if we truly respect one another, if we care for one another, if we love one another, where do we go from here?"

"I don't know. But let's not be too hasty to answer," Danielle responded. "We enjoy where we are. Can we at least tap each other's wine glass, and sip some more?"

"Sure," said William as he lifted his glass. They softly clashed their wine glasses and slowly sipped the cool wine.

"Maybe we need to explore some what ifs, just like the generals do during their war games and strategy sessions," William suggested.

"Is this a war?" inquired Danielle.

"Maybe a war of hearts and of emotions, between two of the most enlightened minds in Washington."

They both laughed.

"Is that a serious joke, William?" Danielle coyly asked.

"Maybe, but I don't think so. Do you?" he asked.

"Without tension, there is no life. With the level of emotional and personal tension on the table, this must be the ultimate in life," Danielle offered.

They looked longingly, intently, with sincere smiles on their faces as they reflected on the tension that Danielle had described and that they both were feeling.

William said, "Danielle, if you could do anything in the world right now, what would it be?"

She smiled, "Make love to you, right now."

"Danielle!" William exclaimed, caught by surprise, but perhaps he had asked for it. Danielle and he had connected before, many times. This was one of those times.

"Sounds great," he continued on. "Your place or mine?" he asked.

"Very funny," she said. "How about mine?"

He laughed. "Fine."

Both knew that wasn't appropriate or possible.

"Don't you have any qualms at all, Danielle, about what we are talking about? Especially after our earlier conversation regarding love and fairness, truthfulness and responsibility?"

"Yes. I have qualms. And I am trying to think them through. I must be sensitive to my feelings and my emotions. And I feel very strongly and very emotionally about you. I am most conscious of our serious discussions about love, responsibility, truthfulness, and fairness. Fairness to ourselves individually and collectively. Fairness and love towards Robert, who I do love. It is just that I don't feel that passionate about Robert. I do feel passionate towards you. I am moved towards you, and I sense you are moved to me."

"I am moved to you, Danielle."

"Then what are we to do?" she asked.

"We do what we must."

"And what is that?" she inquired.

"Each of us must decide."

She disliked this situation. She felt very uncomfortable. But she knew that was only appropriate. She had made every decision herself to get where she was. She and Robert had married many years ago. And that was a rational as well as emotional courtship. And the marriage was fortunate and good for both of them. It had given them strength and support as they built their respective careers. They had many enjoyable moments together and were happy together. But they weren't passionately in love now. Danielle had wondered if they ever would be passionately in love as they once were. Maybe that is why she had thought so often recently about whether she, whether they, ought to have a baby while she still could. She knew it was a decision that they had to make in the next year or two. Was she ready? Is that what she really wanted? Did Robert really want it? He said "okay with him," but how did he really feel? For a cardiologist and a man close to the heart, one would expect him to be more passionate.

70

Perhaps she should have the baby with William. My God, that was a wild thought! William, single? Or William, married? That was another crazy thought! Why were all these crazy thoughts coming to her now? Was it because she was nearing forty? Was it because she didn't really know where she stood with Robert?

She knew how she felt about William, but how did William really feel? Was he just missing his wife and a companion? Was Danielle the ideal woman for him, or merely a safe, convenient friend? He was handsome, bright and powerful. Many women would give anything for him.

"Danielle?" he interrupted.

"Yes, William?"

"Are we done with lunch?" he asked.

"Yes, of course."

It was a strange answer. It was a strange feeling that Danielle was sensing.

"All paid up," William said as he stood first.

Danielle was in a trance. She sensed William close by, but Danielle was wrestling within herself. Her consciousness, her sensitivities were finding her present in this restaurant, then at home, alone, and then with Robert. And then she was back here in this restaurant, very close to the Senator and then proceeding towards the sun outside.

The fresh air felt good, she said to herself, as a light summer breeze cooled the intense heat of the July day.

She turned to William, and he to her, and instantly they moved towards each other and embraced. They kissed passionately, right outside The Hawk and Dove restaurant door, oblivious to anyone around them. They stopped kissing long enough to grasp each other more fully in a full-body hug, pulling each other closer, tighter than before. She felt his powerful left hand in the middle of her back, his right hand cupped under her left arm and brushing her bosom on that side. She placed her right hand on his left shoulder blade and her left hand at the base of his spine. How she wanted to take off his clothes and to be with him alone in bed. She moved her hands to the front of his body, his chest, and then to either side of his face, as he held her tightly. She squeezed his head, her left hand running through the hair on the back of his head, while her right hand pressed against his cheekbone. They kissed passionately for a while and finally she felt the need to retreat. It was getting too hot. And she just wanted to be held firmly and so did he.

After a fleeting moment, she placed her face against his chest and squeezed him hard, feeling all of him.

Gradually they became aware of the afternoon sun, of the voices passing by, and in the distance, some noise from passing cars.

They released each other's firm grasp and separated. Their sides were still touching as they turned to walk up Pennsylvania Avenue together.

They were slowly walking together when they heard two young girls on roller blades say, "Look at the lovey doveys." Danielle and William laughed. Conscious of their public surroundings, they separated some more, although they still held hands.

Danielle was most sensitive to the crowds. When they neared the Library of Congress, they released their hands. She felt alone again. As she glanced at William, he smiled. He's alone too, Danielle thought, perhaps more alone than I.

"Thank you for that kiss and hug," Danielle said, as her long hair blew in her face.

"You are welcome, Danielle. Thank you for the passionate kiss and meaningful hug."

A chill ran down Danielle's back as she realized she wanted more. She loved William. She passionately loved him and all he stood for. What must he think of me, she thought. What would he think of his wife years ago, if he had seen her kissing another man the way Danielle kissed William? Danielle did not want to focus on that. What would Danielle think or feel if she had seen her Robert kissing another woman, a doctor perhaps, or a nurse, so passionately? Danielle was thinking and feeling so many things.

She wanted to think about William, and looked at him, and thought the ultimate. She smiled. He smiled again. She realized she was following him. Her car was parked in the opposite direction behind the Canon and Rayburn House Office Buildings.

"Where are we going?" she asked.

"Where do you want to go?"

"I don't know, but my car is in a different direction."

"Where is it?"

"It is behind the House Office Building."

"So what do you want to do?" He stopped and looked at her.

Her heart sank. She realized she was on the spot. She only wanted to be with him. Wherever they were.

"What would you like to do?" she asked.

"Do you want to come to my house?"

"Sure, but just for a little while."

"You still have a key, don't you?"

"Yes," she said.

"Well, I will see you there shortly."

William had a beautiful three-bedroom condo in Rosslyn

overlooking the Kennedy Center and Washington, D.C. On a day like today there was a beautiful view of the planes proceeding down the path of the Potomac River and landing at National Airport.

Danielle arrived first at the condo. At the door, she was greeted by Satchmo, William's ten year old black Labrador.

Danielle went in, took her shoes off, sat in the plush couch looking out over Washington. Satchmo jumped up and leaned next to her leg. She was stroking Satchmo when William came in. Satchmo leaped off the couch and into the arms of his master.

"Danielle, how about a hot fudge sundae with whipped cream and nuts?" asked William.

"A hot fudge sundae?"

"Yes," William replied. "We didn't have any dessert at The Hawk and Dove. Or did you forget?"

"I thought we had dessert," Danielle said accenting dessert.

"Very funny," William returned. "Well?"

"Well, okay," she said. "But go easy on the nuts."

"How can I? I am talking about you and me."

"Now it is your turn to be the joker, I see."

A few minutes later, as they were listening to Yanni at the Acropolis on the cassette recorder, William came into the room. "Here, how's this, Danielle?"

"Disgusting," she replied as she used her right index finger to lop off some whipped cream. William had piled on the whipped cream, something he loved to do. They then took turns feeding each other ice cream in a sensual way. William had even added cherries on top.

As they ate the sundaes while sitting on the soft leather couch, with Satchmo on the floor at their feet, William leaned over and kissed Danielle on the lips.

Her cool lips soon warmed up to those of William, and before long, Danielle was passionately kissing him, her cold tongue quickly becoming warm. As she began to mount a more passionate offense, biting and eating his lips, her sundae, held in her left hand, spilled onto his lap, creating a mild cool sensation that quickly backed him off, and had them both laughing hysterically.

"If I wanted the sundae in my lap, I would have made a special request," he loudly stated.

"Here let me get it," she responded as she went to bury her head in his lap.

"Danielle, Danielle," he pleaded. "That's okay, I can scoop it myself." But she playfully insisted, and before long they were rolling on the floor.

Satchmo, a bit startled himself, moved out of the way to a more distant and secure corner of the living room. Danielle and William were now in the middle of the living room floor, passionately embracing, her long hair entangled in his hand, her blouse out of her skirt. She had her hands under his shirt, teasing the hair on his chest and lower back. Within minutes they had removed most of each other's clothing. They were slowly and longingly kissing each other, on the lips, then on each other's neck and chest. Sensations were penetrating each other's body. She moved her hands lower and he did likewise. They slowly pulsated in rhythm, first slowly, and then in faster unison. Each was reaching the heights of pleasure. Danielle could not believe the level of passion she felt. It was so right, so vivid, so transcendingly beautiful. William, passionately feeling Danielle, as he had never felt another woman, tried to be as sensitive, accommodating and responsive as he could. But he felt the full strength of his masculinity, and a rush came. The bolt of heat struck each of them simultaneously. They squeezed each other, and embraced as tightly as two people could entwine themselves. Their bodies tremored from the heat of passion. Sweat was felt in each of their palms, on their foreheads, on their touching bellies, their thighs and the backs of their legs. They felt the heat of their bodies for minutes. Danielle was on fire. William's body started to cool faster. They stroked each other, on their foreheads and around their ears, on each shoulder and down each arm. They ran their fingers across each other's belly, chest and breast. They tingled and laughed and lightly squirmed in each other's arms when sensitive areas were touched.

They lay quietly in ecstasy, stroking each other in sensitive ways, and then rolled towards each other, softly kissing while looking into each other's eyes. They closed their eyes, and then embraced.

First to speak was Danielle. "Thanks for the dessert," she said.

"You are more than welcome, Danielle. I guess I should have gone easier on the whipped cream."

"Or skipped it all together."

"No, if I hadn't given you any ice cream at all, how would you have felt?"

"Probably not too much different than I did. And you know that. But I think you set me up, especially when you kissed me. You knew I was going to drop that ice cream in your lap. You planned that didn't you?"

"Actually no. I thought I might find the whipped cream someplace else."

"Do you put legislation together like that?" she asked.

"Sometimes. I mean we usually include the nuts, we miss the cherries, and may or may not know if we all agree on the amount of whipped cream or type of ice cream," he said.

"There's no place like Washington, D.C."

"No, there isn't. You really do love it, don't you, Danielle? I guess it is because it is the land of love, responsibility, truthfulness and fairness," said William.

"What are you trying to do? Trying to make me feel as guilty and hypocritical as possible at this very positive moment?"

"No, not exactly. I'm just trying to get us to focus on reality. The in-depth discussion we had earlier. The great lunch we had together. The passionate love and sex we enjoyed. And now the cycle returns to our bare selves, vulnerable human beings trying to be the best we can, but perhaps, breaking or at least bending the mores of this perfect life."

"I don't feel guilty," said Danielle. "I feel and felt a passionate love for you. I still love Robert. It obviously is an imperfect love, but I've felt my imperfections before, and whether with Robert or you, I will continue to love you both to the best of my ability."

"Lucky us," said William.

"Who do you mean? You and I, or you and Robert?"

"All of us, I guess."

"That's crazy, isn't it, William? Jean Paul Sartre said life is absurd."

"He also said hell is other people. I don't know if that fits in our case or not."

"Yes. That is strange." They lay side by side on the bed, staring up at the ceiling.

"Love is nurturing. You sure have nurtured me again these last few hours," Danielle said.

"Can't say I don't feel nurtured myself."

"But will we be nurtured for minutes, hours, days, years,

or a lifetime?" asked Danielle.

"We've been nurturing each other for hours, days, months and years so far," William said.

"That we have," Danielle reflected. "You know we listen so well to each other. We can communicate on so many levels. I feel your compassion towards me and I feel you are supportive of me. William do you feel similarly about me?"

"Yes. You listen very well. We hear each other and can pick up a conversation anytime and anywhere. I felt your compassion very much today. But I have felt it when I am not with you. Like the past week or two. I know you are supportive of me. Whether it is politically, intellectually, or personally."

"Few people have what we have. Do you know that?" Danielle asked.

"I know."

"And you know what else?"

"What?"

"We try very hard to live the truth. To recognize it, appreciate it and live it. It is like the paradigm of our relationship. You know I love Robert. But I love you too. How could I not respond to the truth I felt within myself, of my feelings for you? How could I not recognize that and appreciate it? It was like your call to me to meet you for lunch. Or your call to me regarding anything at any time. How can I not respond to that truthful feeling within me to respond positively to you. It is just like Robert calling me. You know I would respond to him however I can. He knows that. It is just that there are these societal constraints, except for the Mormons with their many wives. I am trying to respond as well as I can to the call or sound from each of you. You must think I am crazy sharing all of this out loud with you," said Danielle.

"I am glad you did."

"And being fair to all people, and equitable and evenhanded." Danielle turned away from William and asked, "Am I being fair and equitable and evenhanded with you and Robert?" She turned quickly to face William.

"I guess you are, Danielle. I cannot speak for Robert."

"You guess I am?" She turned from him again. I need to reflect further on this, she said to herself. I feel I am fair but am I kidding myself? Where does my true loyalty lie?

William stared at her as she turned back towards him. She continued. "I am trying to be responsible for myself. Responsible to you. Responsible to Robert. It is not perfect responsibility. But I am trying to be responsible. I care for you. I care for Robert. I care for myself. Or else I wouldn't be here with you, feeling so good. I respect your rights. But you did invite me into your home to share the rights you enjoy. I do try hard to respect the rights of Robert. But I am troubled by the rights and commitment of our marriage and his rights to the marriage as he understands them. I have stretched these rights of marriage. But, I love you, William. I love and respect you very much." Tears ran down her cheek.

William held her for a long time. "I love you too, Danielle."

Chapter 4
Be Respectful

Several weeks later on July 31st, Danielle and Robert were packing for their two week vacation in Colorado. They hadn't taken two weeks together in years. They had taken a week here and there, at Christmas or New Year's, and had spent long weekends together in the fall or spring. But two weeks was a real luxury.

A friend of theirs had offered his large townhouse at Arrowhead, just outside of Beaver Creek, about one hundred and twenty miles from Denver. Arrowhead was advertised as Vail's private address. It was a beautiful stretch of land right off Colorado's Interstate 70. It had a great private golf course as well as a quad ski lift to Arrowhead Mountain. The beauty and legacy of the area had been enhanced by a recent purchase by Vail Associates, now connecting Arrowhead and Beaver Creek mountains with Vail mountain. Situated at an elevation of seventy-five hundred feet, the days there were gorgeous in the summertime, usually eighty to ninety degrees temperature without any humidity. Night temperatures dropped into the fifties, forties and thirties. Danielle and Robert were really looking forward to this vacation. The Vail Valley was a great place to shop with beautiful antique shops, art galleries, craft shops, exclusive clothing stores and boutiques and a wide variety of excellent restaurants. There was horseback riding at several places nearby including right above the Hyatt Regency hotel in Beaver Creek. Their friends had also told them to take the balloon rides that originated on the Arrowhead Mountain property and to go mountain climbing and back packing in the Arrowhead, Beaver

Creek and Vail Mountains.

The thought of having a stimulating summer vacation in the Colorado Mountains was refreshing enough. Add to that the local Rochester Philharmonic at the Gerald Ford Theater, the Joffrey Ballet and a variety of music entertainment there and at Beaver Creek, and one had the makings of an ideal time.

"Robert, I am really looking forward to our vacation together," Danielle said.

"I am too. It has been a very busy year. And to think we will have two weeks together."

Both were elated to be leaving the everyday workings of Washington, D.C. For Robert it had been a demanding year. With a constantly growing practice and significant health care delivery changes, even without a Congressionally passed health reform legislation, Robert was faced with as much stress as any physician in America. He was inspired by new developments in an ever-evolving cardiology practice and like most cardiologists was always up to the challenges of the day. He had worked long and hard these last seven months, with rewarding results.

Danielle had also worked as hard and as long as any year since college. She found the health reform debates both exhilarating and frustrating. The longer the discussion lasted the hotter the conflicts became, the more she lost hope for the passage of any significant health reform legislation this year.

Danielle had felt from the beginning that Jackson's health care plan was too complex and controversial. It had locked out too many important players in the debate and for too long. Danielle and Senator Hart had discussed this often for hours at a time. Despite the assistance of several women Senators and Representatives including Senator Diane Kowalski of Maryland and Senator Barbara Goldberg of California, Congresswoman

Bonnie Carter of Maryland and Julie Taft of California, a multitude of special interests had developed effective grass roots and advertising campaigns against the plan. Congressional personalities like Senator Toynbee, Chair of the Senate Finance Committee; Congressman Bob Turk, of the Ways and Means Committee; Congressman John Waddell; and other key Democratic leaders were not involved from the beginning as they should have been. Republican leaders like Senator Pete Drake, Congressman Ken Williamson and Fred Johnson in the House also felt slighted. The continuing cost and budget concerns of health reform were not properly anticipated and addressed. And that confusion, fed by opposing self interests, created greater ambivalence and concern by the American public.

Danielle and Senator Hart had discussed all of this intensely over the past year and a half. Those professional discussions, seen similarly by the two, had increased the personal closeness of Danielle and the Senator. That had also weighed psychologically heavy on Danielle and aggravated the stress she was feeling inwardly as August drew near.

Danielle would have more time while vacationing with Robert, to evaluate her personal life, in particular the marriage. While Danielle exercised religiously every week, she had not focused enough on herself and her relationship to Robert. These two weeks would allow her that luxury of thought.

Now packed, Robert and Danielle left for the airport on the morning of August 1, destined for Denver where they would get a convertible rent-a-car for the two hour drive to Arrowhead.

On the three and a half hour plane ride west, Danielle worked on her year-long project. Danielle had read Steve Covey's Seven Habits of Highly Effective People, Bill Bennett's Book of Virtues and other best sellers like Scott Peck's Road Less Traveled

and Further Along the Road Less Traveled as well as Thomas
Moore's Care of the Soul. Friends in business, especially those
involved in world and international affairs, had recommended
books that dealt with values and principles that affected America
and the world. She had read Russ Kidder's Shared Visions in a
Troubled World and James Liebig's Merchants of Vision. She had
also read other recent popular management books by Ken
Blanchard and Vincent Peale on Ethical Management and Peter
Senge's Fifth Discipline. Danielle had the opportunity to meet and
talk with Bob Rosen and then read his book on The Healthy
Company. She even had gone back to read a book her father had
sent her years back, Robert Fulghum's Everything I Ever Learned,
I Learned in Kindergarten. Danielle was ever-vigilant to read
anything that seemed to be popular and reflected world opinion or
key concepts and values that were important to people. She read
an interesting article by a Japanese researcher, Sato, who
contrasted key and significant words of the Japanese people of the
past few decades. All of these readings gave Danielle a keener
insight into what principles might best underlie her own world in
this rapidly changing universe with all of its diversions and
stresses.

One aspect of this reflection had bothered Danielle. Most
of the significant readings were by men. Surely there were
significant writings by women regarding fundamental values and
principles of life today. Kidder and Liebig quoted or referred to
various female leaders from places as diverse as Mozambique and
China. Mother Teresa, perhaps the greatest twentieth century
example of a legacy of love, wrote nine books.

Danielle was fortunate to have heard about the writings of
Hazel Henderson. In fact, perhaps one of the best and most
illuminating insights came from Hazel's 1991 book, Paradigms in

Progress, where she presented a philosophy that addressed post industrial society. While the flight attendant served her coffee, Danielle pulled Hazel's book out of her travel bag.

Danielle was focusing today on the concepts of respect for life, freedom and unity. Hazel was illuminating on all three. Regarding respect for life, for instance, she emphasized how we needed to invest in people, the true 'Wealth of Nations.' She also commented on the fragility of human life and how each of us needed to search for inner satisfaction and personal growth and help others to do likewise.

Regarding freedom, Hazel was quite refreshing, stating that we needed a clearer shopping guide for a better world for all people, rather than just focusing on the narrow and self centered lifestyles of the rich and famous. She called for more systematic reconceptualizing and redesign of our communities and the true definition of communities rather than relying on limited technological fixes in our everyday life. Also symbolic of the twentieth and twenty first centuries, Hazel emphasized the greening of the world, with the rise and growth of green parties and movements throughout the world, in sharp contrast to the low environmental concern of previous generations.

What an optimistic viewpoint, Danielle thought as she read Hazel's thoughts. "Robert, let me share something of real beauty with you. You know how we recently discussed the fundamental principles and values underlying our actions such as love, responsibility, truthfulness and fairness? Let me share some thoughts regarding these concepts and others regarding respect for life, freedom and unity." Here Danielle went on to share the thoughts of Hazel Henderson in her Paradigms in Progress with Robert.

"That's terrific," he said. "Danielle you ought to combine

that with all those other readings you've been doing in the past year and lay out a modern day mosaic of human values."

"That's exactly what I am planning to do," Danielle responded.

It was around noon when they landed in Denver. It was one of those glorious summer days in Colorado. Near 80 degrees in temperature, sun shining ever so brightly against a very clear and blue sky. In the distance there were those white puff clouds, like cotton balls hanging over the mountain range in the West.

Danielle and Robert walked the long terminal path towards baggage. As they walked they peered out the windows, the stunning Colorado weather beckoning them. The wait for their bags seemed like an eternity, so anxious were they to get going. Finally with bags in tow, they went out and boarded the van to their rental car, a Chrysler Sebring convertible.

Now they were on the highway, Route 70 West.

On their left was the beautiful skyline of downtown Denver. They crossed Interstate 25 and continued west to the exhilarating Rocky Mountains. The ride was beautiful. It was always beautiful regardless of the weather. Danielle was always uplifted by the ride through the mountains. She looked out the window with all the interest of a small child in a candy store. Eyes open wide. She was awed by the majesty of the mountains, with their impressive shapes and provoking jagged edges protruding into the sky. At their base, between the mountains and the Interstate, was the cool crackling and roaring creek of mountain spring water. The sunlight glistened upon the waves and streaming water, as the car circled the curvaceous mountain path, up to eight thousand feet and higher. They passed through the sleepy village of Georgetown, which reminded her of another Georgetown and the Potomac River along the banks of

Washington, D.C. and Northern Virginia. Despite these fond memories of home, Danielle was glad to be in Colorado, away from the hustle and bustle of Washington, the city of power mongers, high roll politicians, CEOs and ambassadors, and the other bright and ambitious people of that area. Now it was just Danielle and Robert in a convertible climbing the beautiful Rockies.

As she viewed the extraordinary scenery along the Interstate she thought how fortunate she was to be driving along this gorgeous stretch of nature with a man who loved her. She also thought of all those in the United States and other parts of the world who would never have this good fortune. It was so unlike other highways around the big cities of the Northeast, Boston, New York, Philadelphia and Baltimore. So many children and adults of those cities would never enjoy the beautiful journey that Danielle and Robert were taking this afternoon. Danielle thought of Bobby Kennedy and his empathy and desire for those less fortunate and remembered his speech, "I see things and ask why not?" Why couldn't those poor children and adults have the opportunity to see these Rockies? Ever the idealist, Danielle started thinking how it could be arranged for those people to be sponsored in bus and train trips to see the great Rockies. But why was Danielle thinking of such issues? She needed to think beautiful positive thoughts. Danielle was not going to solve health care reform or other social and cultural engineering this afternoon. No, she and Robert needed to enjoy the present and be in awe and wonder and at peace. At a later date, she and Robert could develop solutions to these social shortcomings.

Danielle, conscious that she had been in her own little world for a while, turned away from the window and towards Robert. How lucky she was to share her life with Robert, in marriage and on this overdue vacation.

"Robert, it's great to be with you," she said as she stared at him driving and tried to bring herself back to the present moment. "It's great to be with you Danielle. Isn't this an unbelievable day? We couldn't be more fortunate."

"It is truly unbelievable. No matter how much I am exposed to it, I am always struck by the beauty and impressiveness of it all. It gives you a great respect for nature. A respect for the awesome power of the mountains. The beauty of the trees, the creek, the variety and size and different shapes of the mountains. The exhilarating feeling of ascending in a man-made car on a man-made highway to see ever more impressive views of a day in the mountains. It is so incredible."

"It is all the more incredible when you realize we have the freedom to take this or any other route and explore all this natural beauty. And if we want to stop to sit by the stream at the base of the mountain, to have a picnic, or climb up the mountain we can. It is so gorgeous," Robert remarked.

"It gives you a different perspective on our everyday life," Danielle said. "It makes you appreciate other beauty in our everyday lives, like the respect and beauty of human relationships. Of our relationship to our surroundings whether today here in these mountains, or yesterday for you and me and our lives in Washington, D.C. How fortunate we are to be able to transcend our everyday lives, to have this ability to reflect on what we have, who we are and where we are going. Why can't everyone come to Colorado?"

Robert laughed. "I am sure as much as the residents of Colorado love it here, and want some people to visit, they sure wouldn't want the world to come here."

"Well why not? I think everyone deserves a little

Colorado. It makes me think of that great sweatshirt 'Wish you were beautiful. Colorado is here.'"

"There is an incredible freedom one feels here. It is like no other feeling I know. You feel like the eagle out there floating among the peaks of the Rockies. Not a care in the world. You are beyond the convertible we are in. You fly and float with the wind under your wings bringing you to ever higher levels. And you bend a little to the left and a little to the right and then you dip down and then you soar up. Such an unbelievable feeling. Can't you just feel the pull of the mountains and the skies?"

"Yes. And I love it. An incredible feeling of freedom, far from the cares of the everyday world. No ties, no meetings, no phones ringing, no faxes, no being late. It's like you are always on time. Your time. Your own time. The freedom from time. Except for day and night, you lose all consciousness of time. The days and nights in the mountains are things of beauty. So are the sunrises and sunsets. I can hardly wait for today's sunset and tomorrow's sunrise."

It was early afternoon. They had just passed through Loveland Pass, the highest point on the journey to Arrowhead. Coming through the Eisenhower Tunnel, a superb architectural masterpiece that cut through three miles of mountains, they headed west to Lake Dillon and Silverthorne. One had to consciously test the brakes of the car because the slope downhill was quite steep, and one picks up speed similar to a downhill skier. Periodically they encountered designed pathways that veered to the right and sloped uphill for use by runaway trucks.

"Robert, aren't you always amazed at the runaway paths?"

"Yes, they are incredible. I would love to have an echocardiographic tape of a truck driver's heart who has lost control of his vehicle and made the split-second decision to run his

88

semi up the sand pebble path."

"How often do you think it occurs?"

"On an icy or rainy night maybe a couple of times. On a clear day like today, probably not at all unless the truck driver has fallen asleep, is on drugs or otherwise not in full control of his faculties."

"It has to be an incredible feeling when you are out of control."

"It probably is similar to any one of us who has stretched his own limits, gone beyond moderation, beyond the reasonable, and lost control."

"There is probably a higher percentage of us in Washington, D.C. who have lost control of our lives, than truck drivers who have used the runaway paths."

"Probably a similar percentage," said Robert laughing.

"I think we don't truly appreciate freedom, freedom to drive anywhere, freedom to breathe, freedom to practice medicine, freedom to politically negotiate, freedom to lobby, freedom to live wherever we want."

"You mean freedom to do anything?"

"What does freedom mean to you?" Danielle inquired.

"Oh, my goodness, Danielle. It means so many things. I think oftentimes we don't truly realize that freedom is linked to accountability. One can be free as long as they are accountable to others, responsible to oneself, one's loved ones, one's community, one's world."

"Robert, I think it means to foster human creativity, to make a meaningful contribution, to appreciate one's creative ability, like the bird's ability to be free, to fly where it wants, as long as it does not injure others."

"I think freedom is our ability to take a vacation. To be

free of our everyday professional commitments. Free to visit
Colorado. To enjoy this glorious day."

"I feel freedom in our opportunity to self renew these two
weeks. To find out who we are, and renew our individual spirits
as well as our unified spirit as a couple."

"Don't you just love our independence, Danielle? Our
ability to develop our individuality, while at the same time
developing our relationship together."

"Free to be you and me."

"Yes, free to be you and me. I love you, Danielle."

"I love you too, Robert." Danielle looked lovingly at him,
yet felt an empty feeling as her mind and spirit turned to thoughts
of William and Barry.

"Danielle. Danielle," Robert repeated.

Danielle had drifted away.

"Yes, Robert."

"What were you thinking?"

"Oh, nothing," she recovered. "Just thinking of how
touching your comments were." She turned to him and smiled.

He smiled back.

"Robert, did it take courage to say that or did it just flow
naturally?"

"It just came naturally, Danielle. But it probably took
some courage, because I know I don't always say it to you. Yet I
feel it often for you. I take a lot for granted in everyday life. We
don't stop to reflect as we should. Or share our love with
someone."

"I love you too, Robert. I appreciate your saying it and
sharing it with me. It is a very loving thing to do. I am as caught
up in the everyday as you. You have such a dedication to your
practice, your patients, your students and your colleagues. And

probably, no, definitely your nurses and other health team members. Robert?"

"Yes, Danielle?"

"Have you ever had an affair with one of your nurses?"

"Danielle, are you serious?"

"Yes, I am serious. How about a physician, colleague or some other attractive woman you met in your office?"

"Danielle, the only women I have shared anything intimate with was long before you and I met. Why do you ask?"

"I was just thinking of our discussion on freedom and our comments about being free to be you and me. And I was thinking of the freedom you have in your ordinary day. And the freedom of others who run into you in a normal day. And your freedom to be with them. That's all."

"Okay." Robert was tempted to ask Danielle the same thing. Had she had any affairs since they were married eight years ago. But he decided against it.

"Don't you feel empowered, Robert, when you are free?"

"Yes, I think that the true beauty of freedom is the feeling of power it produces within us. Empowerment is both an underused and an overused word today. Overused in the sense that everyone talks about empowerment and empowering others. But very few of us provide meaningful insight into empowerment and how to become empowered. Freedom and empowerment go hand in hand. We need to teach people to be free and to be empowered to realize their full potential as human beings."

"Robert, you must realize it as much as anyone. You deal with the full power of one's heart, probably our most sacred possession, next to our brain."

"Greater than one's brain my dear."

"Is it? Why?"

"Well, it all depends on whether you buy into the theory of ordo amoris, the order of the heart. Many of us have been trained to believe that there is a higher order of the heart that matches the higher order of human beings."

"Now that is chauvinistic, Robert. Isn't it? We have discussed this before."

"Yes but never conclusively," he said. They both laughed. Danielle recalled their first meeting in Washington, D.C. She was a lobbyist with the AMA. They met at Georgetown Medical School's Open House for the new Heart House expansion at the University. Danielle was invited by a good friend of hers, Gabrielle Kenney, married to a distinguished Georgetown cardiologist. Danielle and Robert were taken with each other at first sight. And they had a similar discussion then, a decade ago, about the meaning of the heart and ordo amoris.

"There is a balance and a rhythm to the heart, that parallels the balance and rhythm of freedom," Robert remarked as their Chrysler neared the towns of Lake Dillon and Frisco. "Freedom has its limits just as the heart does. We are learning more all the time about the stresses of the heart, which are similar to the stresses of freedom. Danielle, you know all about the stresses to the Constitution, to the Congress, to the President, to every campaign and election that transpires in our democracy. That's why we have the balance of power among the judicial, legislative, and executive branches."

"You are very right, Robert. As you always are," she remarked with a loving smile.

"Do you want to stop here and get a drink, maybe shop at the outlets?"

"Sounds like a great idea. I wanted to send my mother some glassware and this is a great place to look."

92

Robert cut off the highway to the right. Silverthorne and Dillon had a great combination of outlet shops, over 100 of them on either side of Interstate 70.

Robert and Danielle decided to stop at Dairy Queen, an old favorite of theirs. Nothing like a balanced lunch with a hot fudge brownie.

After lunch, Robert and Danielle decided to hit the shops on the Silverthorne side first. Danielle wanted to go to the Mikasa shop.

"Danielle, there is a book store in the corner. I am going to head over there while you are in Mikasa."

Robert was looking for some interesting reading on Colorado and its natural beauty as well as an historical biography. As he browsed around he heard someone from his left say, "Doctor Robert Anderson?"

He turned quickly and noticed an attractive blond facing him. "Yes, I am Robert Anderson."

"Hello. I am Dr. Bailey Trudeau. I heard you speak at last year's American Heart Association's Annual Meeting in San Francisco. I was quite impressed."

Robert, positively taken back, responded, "Well thank you very much. Are you a cardiologist?"

"Yes. I practice in Vancouver, but I own a house in Arrowhead near Beaver Creek, about an hour away."

"Yes, I know where it is. I am headed there myself."

"You are?"

"Yes, I am."

"Are you a golfer?"

"Yes. I enjoy it. I only wish I had more time for it. Do you golf as well?"

"Yes. I've belonged to Arrowhead since 1990, and if I

hadn't fallen in love with cardiology, I might be playing professionally."

"You're that good?"

"Well, at one time, I was quite good. About an eight handicap right now. In Vancouver, it is tough to golf in the winter time."

"An eight handicap is quite good," Robert responded.

"And you, what is your handicap?" Bailey inquired with a serious movement of her right eyebrow, as if she was hustling Robert for a game.

Robert hesitated a moment, jokingly thinking the handicap was his wife. "Oh, I am about a ten now," he remarked.

"Well, we could probably play even and I could learn a thing or two about cardiology."

"I would want the shot a side, just to make it even," Robert retorted.

"Sure, if you used the blue tees," Bailey said.

"Robert," Danielle yelled out as she entered the store.

Robert quickly turned, to respond to Danielle. "I ran into a fellow Arrowhead neighbor," Robert informed Danielle.

"Oh, how interesting," Danielle responded with some concern as she sized up the attractive blond.

"Dr. Bailey Trudeau, this is my wife Danielle DiCarlo."

"Pleasure to meet you, Danielle," Bailey remarked holding out her hand.

"My pleasure," Danielle said, reaching to shake Bailey's firm grasp.

"If you care to get together to play golf at Arrowhead, call me. I am listed in the directory. Perhaps we could have a drink," Bailey offered.

"Sounds good. Perhaps we can," Robert responded with

interest.

"Yes, we appreciate the offer," Danielle remarked less inclined and wondering about the chance encounter.

"I enjoyed seeing you again, Robert," Bailey confidently stated. "A pleasure to meet you Danielle."

Enjoyed seeing you again. Where and when had the two met before? "She's gorgeous," Danielle remarked as Bailey exited the store.

"She's a cardiologist from Vancouver and apparently heard me speak in San Francisco," Robert chimed in.

"Oh," Danielle commented. "Did you find something of interest here?" Danielle inquired of her confident husband.

"As a matter of fact I did," he exclaimed as each looked pointedly at one another. "This one on Colorado beauty looks like a fascinating read. Plus I found an interesting book on the first Governor of Colorado."

"I am sure he was an interesting fellow," Danielle commented.

"You probably would find some interesting and insightful side to the Teddy Roosevelt double. Trailblazer, you know."

Danielle and Robert again exchanged those piercing looks when neither needs to state a word, but each understands the other.

It was nearing three o'clock in the afternoon when Danielle and Robert decided to move on. They were only forty-five minutes out of Arrowhead and they knew that the destination would have its own rewards.

The ride between Dillon/Silverthorne and Arrowhead was a gorgeous one, with Lake Dillon on the left, and the afternoon sun glistening on the water. A breathtaking panorama of mountain ranges surrounded the serene lake. Shadows of the mountains to the west and south began to set on the Interstate. Cotton ball clouds amidst the bright blue sky slowly crossed along the horizon. A little creek along the east side of the Interstate added to the perfect afternoon. Just before Copper Mountain, the road jogged in and out among the awesome mountain views.

Danielle was moved to speak. "It is at times like these, when confronted with such natural beauty, that it is hard to deny there is a God. If nothing else, it is an incredible feeling to see such beauty and feel unique transcendent flows within one's spirit. One feels swept along a river flowing with unmatched expectation and delight."

"I agree," Robert responded. The ski trails emblazoned on Copper Mountain made it stick out like a painting in an art gallery. Although it was now summer and there was no snow on the trails, the green of the evergreen trees contrasted with grass-green ski trails. A beautiful sight indeed. Further along the highway towards Vail Pass, there was a unique winding bike path, hundreds of yards below the Interstate and a crackling creek beside it.

"Wow this is incredible," Danielle said.

"Yes, it is."

"Freedom yells out as one breathes in the exhilarating mountain air and feels the awesomeness of God's Rocky Mountains. How can one not respect life when one encounters such beauty. Hundreds of thousands of evergreen trees, the creek, the man-made bike path, blue skies, cotton ball puffs of clouds, a glorious sun warming us as we wind around the mountain. The unity of the mountain mosaic is unmatched," Danielle said.

"Yes it is grand."

Robert and Danielle were united in the freedom and respect for human nature that they experienced that summer afternoon near Arrowhead.

They were on a downhill slope, doing eighty miles an hour

in the Sebring convertible when they spotted the first sign to East Vail, a quaint little village, Vail's closest address to Denver, about one hundred and five miles away. It consisted of condominiums, a smattering of single family homes, and lots of greenery.

A few miles around the bend, was a beautiful golf course carved at the foot of the mountain. Vail Country Club, the original home of the Gerald Ford Invitational Golf Tournament. President Ford, a resident of the Valley, and his supporters had contributed greatly to Vail's expanding culture with, among other things, the Gerald Ford Amphitheater which served as home to some wonderful summer music and arts, including a foot-stomping July Fourth music festival.

Once near the Ford Amphitheater, Danielle and Robert enjoyed their view of the beautiful Vail ski slopes. Vail was a fascinating town with a European ambiance and plenty of shops and restaurants. In the summer it was an unknown treasure, much quieter than its hectic winter schedule, but home to a beautiful setting with warm days and cool nights, a welcome relief for Danielle and Robert.

Recently Vail, Beaver Creek and Arrowhead were interconnected offering the most extended ski areas in the world. Beaver Creek, at the base of Beaver Creek Mountain, had a winding entrance that offered several miles of breathtaking scenery through a divide and a golf course set among the majestic mountains. Houses there ranged in price from three hundred thousand dollars to twelve million.

Robert made a right at the entrance to Beaver Creek, and after driving two and a half miles, arrived at Arrowhead, a smaller, more exclusive neighborhood than either Beaver Creek or Vail. It had a security gate, a Nicklaus- designed golf course, and houses that were worth up to several million dollars.

It was four o'clock. The sun, radiated from the west across the golf course. The road was lined with wild flowers. Danielle and Robert drove past the clubhouse at the base of the mountain. Their four- bedroom townhouse was a quarter of a mile away. It was an end unit with a fifteen-foot window facing the mountain. In the back, there was a Jacuzzi with views of million dollar homes down the mountain. As they brought their luggage in the front door, they saw a deer's head mounted on the wall, as well as various other western knick knacks and native American pictures. In the dining room a giant dream catcher hung on the wall. The kitchen had oak cabinets and a long counter top that circled the kitchen. The living room had a stone fireplace. All rooms had breathtaking mountain views.

"I guess we have arrived," Danielle sighed.

"There are worse places on earth," Robert remarked. "But we won't have to worry about that just now."

It would be easy for Danielle and Robert to feel free in this environment, focus on their respect for life and the unity of their marriage.

***

After a quiet evening at home before the fireplace, with a home-cooked spaghetti dinner, garlic bread, soothing Chardonnay, and a restful mountain sleep, Danielle and Robert awoke early. As they peered out the window they noticed magnificent, multi-colored hot air balloons rising quickly from the Arrowhead property.

Danielle commented, "Just the sight to make your spirit soar."

"Gorgeous," Robert concurred.

98

"We will have to do that one of these mornings."

"Do you think you can tolerate the cool morning air and risk your life in those balloons?" inquired the conservative cardiologist.

"Absolutely. It would be a pleasure."

"Do you want to drive down to where the hot air balloons are taking off?"

"Definitely, let's go."

Wasn't exactly what Robert had in mind for his first morning here, but he always knew what excited and inspired Danielle.

They threw on jeans, deck shoes and sweatshirts, raced down the stairs, and rode their Sebring to Eagle River, where the hot air balloons were.

First out of the car, Danielle had her camera in tow. She ran across the parking lot and began taking a series of pictures. First a picture of those setting up their hot air balloons, carefully stretching out the rubber along the meadow, and minding the strings to avoid intertwining. The captain of each balloon monitored the set-up by his or her assistants. Each balloon had a wooden enclosed porch for about three to four people including the captain. Hot air was pumped in by fiery torches, and the balloons blew up to be several stories high. Their rapid ascent took Danielle's breath away.

Danielle snapped pictures each step of the way, from the layout setup, to the initial ascent and accelerated rise into the bright morning skies.

On subsequent days, Danielle caught pictures of hot air balloons that could not properly take off because of poor wind conditions. She also captured balloons in their descent and final landing.

As she reflected on this beautiful Colorado morning and gained new respect for the art of hot air ballooning, she also thought about showing more respect for life and all that was living.

Chapter 5
Vision and Envision

Back at the townhouse, Danielle and Robert were having a relaxing breakfast. Though it was a bit brisk as the summer mornings in the mountains were, they decided to have their heart-healthy breakfast on the front porch. With well manicured deeply rich grass in the yard, the deck on the hill outside their breakfast nook was a great place to sit at any time of the day.

"Robert, could you live here year-round and practice your cardiology in the mountains?" Danielle inquired.

"Oh, maybe. I never really thought about it before."

"No, I am serious. As you visioned your professional life in cardiology, could you, would you consider living and practicing here?"

"I really would need to think about it, Danielle. I have been fairly fortunate in the opportunities from college on, in pursuing something intellectually stimulating, personally rewarding, with people I have enjoyed working with. As you know Danielle, when you work in the health industry, an essential part of the inspiration is that you feel and know that you are doing good for others. I am sure I could adjust to a productive practice here in the mountains, but the research environment would be more limiting and I wouldn't have the stimulation of the medical students."

Robert continued, "When I think about it, and I haven't for a while, I am as flexible today as I was in Illinois. I was relatively close to my folks, they were great teachers, very good people. They did a lot of good for many people. They were successful professionally and enjoyed very full lives. So part of the reason I went to the University of Illinois was to be close to home. The University was a major state institution, had a diverse and rich faculty and curriculum."

"What did you major in your undergraduate studies, physics and biology?"

"Physics and psychology actually."

"Psychology. That's right. I remember when we first started dating that you and I explored psychology. You often psychoanalyzed my comments and thoughts. You still do."

"Everyone must have their leisure pursuits, Danielle," Robert chided.

"So, professionally, how did you decide on a career in cardiology?"

"Actually, at Illinois I very much enjoyed my studies and interactions with my classmates. Because my father was an internist, trained at Stanford, with a double major in physics and psychology from DePaul, I guess it was in my genes to pursue a career in medicine. And as you know cardiology is a subspecialty of internal medicine, so in some ways I took my father's studies to the next level of sub-specialization. I loved the sun, so I went to medical school at the University of Florida, which was said to have a great cardiology department. Always looking to test the limits, I moved on to the University of California at San Francisco which also had a great tradition in cardiology. The cross country shift to the Nation's capital was a gradual one. I went to the University of Chicago to teach because of its traditions, its research orientation, and again it was close to my family. My brothers, one an internist and the second an attorney, lived there with their families and my sister lived down-state where she taught and was involved in research in psychology and anthropology. Chicago was a great place to live."

"But not great enough to hold you."

"Well, when Sergio Ballisteros was recruited from Spain as chair for the Cardiology Department, I knew that Georgetown University was going to be in the midst of very exciting cardiology research, teaching and practice. Here was an individual who challenged the best minds in U.S. cardiology from Harvard and Indiana, to Alabama and California. And he also had a fascinating liberal arts orientation where he was involved in cross discipline studies involving philosophy, theology, psychiatry and applied research."

"Are you telling me you will stay there forever, Robert?"

"Forever is a long time. I think it is difficult to project beyond three to five years, although significant studies have been done over the past ten years, and more developments are planned for the next ten years. But medicine, science and technology are changing at such amazing speeds, it is difficult to see beyond a short horizon. Don't you agree, Danielle?"

"I guess. You and I are probably as conscious of the future as we are of the present. You know of the futurist health work I have been engaged in. Our global interconnectivity, the presence and use of Internet where we can download international data bases from the Far East, Australia, India, Europe, the Mid East, Africa, the Eastern European Countries and Russia, and be in ongoing dialogue with the best minds and practices in the countries. And here at home, with such significant resources as our corporations, universities, associations, and grassroots communities, we can pursue the best health in the world. You know this from your Georgetown, Chicago and San Francisco experiences, as well as the international community you interact with daily like Sergio and others. Look at how your professional and scientific meetings have expanded and the ongoing dialogues you have established over the past two decades."

"I know. It is truly amazing. And to think that I can plug into noontime grand rounds at Georgetown or morning classes at UCSF through the Internet."

"That's what I mean. You can live here at seventy five hundred feet elevation and continue your professional cardiology pursuits."

"Right you are, Danielle. I'll E-mail Sergio now and tell him to call me at his convenience about establishing Georgetown West."

They both laugh.

"But it is a serious joke, Robert."

"The joke is on you, Danielle. You could never isolate yourself here and miss the day in, day out hustle of Washington, D.C. politics and your colleagues there."

"But I wouldn't be isolated here. I could use C Span, TV, the Internet, and phone combined with periodic visits to Washington when Congress was in session."

"Oh, Danielle, you are out of session. You know you would miss your constituency, and colleagues."

"I could do it."

"But for how long? And do you truly want to? You were asking me to reflect on my past, my present and my future. What about you and your professional future? Based on your past and current activities, are you serious about a Rocky Mountain high way of life?"

"I don't know. It is fun to reflect on, don't you think? I, like you, have been quite fortunate. Fortunate to have been born to my talented and dedicated folks. Mom taught and did counseling. She did a tremendous amount of volunteer and social action kinds of things. Fact was, and still is to a degree, that Mom and Dad were always social activists, always trying to help people and improve their community. Dad not only was one of Illinois' most successful state senators, first elected at age twenty seven and majority leader at forty three, he was a successful dad and local leader. In twenty years of state senate activity, he was quite involved in some landmark legislation on education, health, welfare and the state's economy. And then I think of his success as a businessman in insurance and real estate. His real estate developments were written up nationally and internationally. And my parents owe a lot to their parents. Gramma and Grandpa DiCarlo did similar volunteer and social activity, always helping out the down-trodden and making significant contributions to their community, like local schools and churches."

"Yes, it helps to have lineage to the Pope and liberal socially active Catholicism for one's roots."

"So, Christ was a Jew and Mary was a single virgin who gave birth to the king of men and women."

"And we Catholics take credit for the savior and know how to raise money for worthy causes."

"Well, you don't have a monopoly on that. So, Danielle back to the fundamental question, what about the future of your professional career? Colorado could stand some of your social activism. Even people living in this mountain paradise can improve their health."

"And the condition of their hearts, Dr. Anderson," Danielle cutely remarked. "As for me, that's the sixty four thousand dollar question. I really enjoy what I am doing. Women and children need as much help as ever with their health and well-being. How long will I do what I am doing? I don't know. For now it appears it will be at least another two years with this Jackson Administration. But beyond that, it is hard to predict. As you say, to visualize three to five years out is a challenge. For some it is a challenge to see the coming day or week. But, Robert, you know how I have talked about my one hundred to one hundred and twenty year existence. Both you and I know that is quite humanly possible."

"Yes, it is."

"And it is easy for any of us to see a thirty to forty year full time professional life, in several different professions, if we so choose."

"That is so."

"And perhaps another decade, or two or three as a part time professional."

"You and I know how difficult it is to be a part time professional."

"Yes, it is as difficult as being a part time person."

"True."

"But, to continue. If we contemplate that extended full or part time professional life, we can have a very full life."

"Even if we don't preoccupy ourselves or choose such an extended professional life, we can have a very full life."

"That is also true," Danielle concurred.

"Then why don't people have richer lives?"

"Maybe some of us need to enlighten them. They need to take time to reflect on their rich lives."

"Well, isn't that what we essentially are privileged to do with our lives."

"Yes, it is."

"So Danielle, how are you going to enrich your life even greater than it is, to its full potential, now that you are so conscious of your present state of being?"

"Good question. I guess a little more reflection, which is

sorely missing in most people's lives, will illuminate the potential richness that is possible in my life. And your life."

"Yes, in our respective personal and professional lives."

"Robert."

"Danielle."

"Do you want us to have a baby?"

"Do you want a baby?"

"I am considering it."

"Well, then I will consider it."

"Robert, is that the most romantic, most sensual and most inviting proposal you have had to go to bed?"

"I would have to think about it."

"You devil!"

"It is probably the most different proposal I have had. And by a fairly attractive, fairly mature, fairly inviting female."

"It is a rather attractive, sophisticatingly mature and very inviting sensual woman who is making the offer. Do you accept?"

"Are you serious?"

"What do you think?"

"You are arousing the animal in me. Ordo amoris, raging with fire and physical inspiration."

"Well, follow me."

***

A short while later, while laying in their king size bed and reflecting on their consumed union, Danielle says "Thank you, Robert. That was wonderful."

"Yes, it was as satisfying as anytime we have had together."

"Robert."

107

"Yes, Danielle."

"Do you think we made a baby?"

"Did you want a baby?"

"Something in me says yes. And something inside me says no, not yet."

"Well, I think you have a fifty-fifty shot," he surmised "Is it that perfect time of the month?"

"I am not sure. I haven't felt one hundred percent a couple of different times in the last few weeks."

"Well, that is scientific."

"I think I am a little off the mark. But I am off the pill. Did you know?"

"I suspected."

"You did?"

"Yes. You know we have had this discussion a few times over the last few months. And remember when your sister kept prodding you on her visit here. I sensed some family pressure as well as the fact that you are thirty-nine years of age."

"I know. It is an age that I have been most conscious of. Probably accented by a number of women friends who constantly remind me of my few remaining childbearing years. Robert, were you as concerned of being thirty-nine several years back?"

"Well as a male I don't think it bothers us as much as females, maybe partially related to your childbearing years."

"I think that is true. Well what age or ages bother you Robert, or will bother you?"

"Probably eighty-nine."

"Eighty-nine? Why is that?"

"Because my grandmother is eighty-nine and I wonder if I'll outlive her."

"Makes sense. Remember we plan to live to be one

hundred or one hundred and twenty."

"Well, Danielle, what is it? One hundred or one hundred and twenty?"

"One hundred and twenty. How about you?"

"Well at least one hundred. In five years I will let you know if I am half way home or not. Depends on how many children we have by then."

"Are you serious, Robert?"

"Serious, delirious. They say children age you, what do you think?"

"Well having them in our forties, my guess is we will age with children. But in one regard they will keep us young and creative, so that may have it's distinct advantages. How many children do you want to have, Robert?"

"Natural or adopted?"

"Natural first, then adopted."

"Maybe four natural children and two adopted."

"That is pretty specific!"

"I thought you were looking for a quantifiable number. I know how you are always counting the votes."

"But why six, four and two?"

"I don't know. You were odd and I was even. I guess It's like craps."

"So four and two. I guess we'll have to get started, or else there will have to be multiple births."

"Well I do have cousins who are triplets."

"And we have had sets of twins in our family."

"There you are."

"So boys or girls and in what order?"

"What are you, Dunkin' Donuts and you need the order quick? Two and two."

"Two boys and two girls."

"No two sets of twins."

"Now I know you are not being serious."

"Two boys. Two girls. Boy, girl, boy, girl. Matthew, Mark, Luke and John."

"Sounds sort of cute. With you as the father and me as the mother it is easy to see how we would have the four gospels according to the kids."

"Except you are a virgin and my new profession is carpenter."

"Yeah, sure. Sounds cute also, but college tuitions might be tougher to come by."

"Danielle."

"Yes, Robert."

"If Mary had more children than just Jesus, would they all be by Joseph?"

"Good question. I don't know. Do you think our children should be by different fathers?"

"Well, I did say we would adopt two."

All of a sudden, Danielle felt a very distinct chill down her back and exposed legs. She quickly grabbed the covers and covered her legs.

"Did that send a chill down your leg?"

Danielle hesitated. "Yes, as a matter of fact."

"Ah huh. We have pierced your heart. Which comment was it that gave you the stress reaction?"

"You have the data, doctor, please check it."

"It seems to me it was related to the children by a different father. What I am not sure is whether it was specifically related to the adopted children."

"And to think this all began with hot air balloons and

consideration of our professional lives, a conversation that we didn't conclude."

"Do you think we should return to that?"

Danielle rolled over and hugged Robert, a man who seemingly would accept Danielle no matter what role she chose in both her personal and professional lives. He was truly one of a kind. Tall, dark and handsome. Seemingly from royal stock. Very bright. Intellectually stimulating. Well trained. Well mannered. Excellent sense of humor. Excellent human insight. With a good pediatrician's manner. A Perry Mason legal and inquisitive mind. But with the touch of a delicate feather and the warmth of a kindling wood fireplace on Christmas Eve. A very lovable man. Danielle continued to press against him. Head to head. Chest to chest. Pelvis against pelvis. Legs against legs. With arms wrapped around one another. But now in addition to thinking of Robert, she was thinking warmly of William Hart. And Barry! How could she? Her warmest thought was of William. Then she quickly reverted to thinking about and strongly feeling for Robert. And when she looked in his eyes, and he in hers, she got a sinking feeling. Sinking into the arms and body and heart and soul of the man she willingly married eight years ago. And then her mind engaged William and she had a fleeting thought and laughed internally about the dropped ice cream in William's lap. Then she looked back at Robert and they smiled and hugged, and she thought, how can I be so fortunate to have two loving men at the same time. She had no answer other than to feel both of them warmly and intimately. My God, how could she be so lucky and so confused at the same time? And who could she discuss it with? No one, not even her sisters.

They hugged for a long time, adjusting their position ever so gradually when they felt a minor discomfort. Each was engaged in pleasant cuddling, regardless of where their minds wandered.

Chapter Six
Win/Learn: Learn Throughout Life

The next day after a leisurely breakfast, Robert told Danielle he was going for a walk. She was busy with some cleaning and puttering around upstairs and had told him she was going to make some calls back to Washington, D.C. Danielle was forever the consummate professional.

As Robert set out from their townhouse to the east and the rising sun, he spotted Dr. Bailey Trudeau in a magnificently large home on the hill. She looked absolutely ravishing in the early morning sunshine. Her beautiful blond hair was slowly blowing in the mountain breeze. Her silk white and gold jumpsuit clung softly on her shapely body. Robert didn't say anything when he spotted her, merely took in her presence and reminisced about her offer to golf. He wondered if Danielle was included in Bailey's offer. That answer would be forthcoming. He could play it either way. Would Danielle be more suspicious if she wasn't included or if she had the option to decline? How comfortable would it be, the three of them together? And who would ride with whom assuming they all got golf carts? Surely not he and Bailey! Who would be the fourth player? Would Bailey bring a man friend or a girlfriend? Would she ask Robert to get a fourth? Robert didn't know anyone at Arrowhead. How long had Bailey lived here? How much time did she spend here? Robert remembered Danielle's prodding him about having a cardiology practice here. He imagined having Bailey as a cardiology partner, and laughed to himself. Danielle would love it!

By this time he was within two hundred yards of Bailey's million dollar home. She had spotted him as well. He waited for her to speak first.

"Robert, how are you this morning?"

"Terrific, how about yourself?"

"How could anyone be but wonderful on such a glorious morning," she replied. "Would you care for a cup of coffee or orange juice?"

He hesitated and wondered how Danielle would love this. "Sure, I'll have an orange juice." Safe enough, he thought, probably on Bailey's deck overlooking the golf course. He walked across her beautifully manicured backyard. "Your yard is beautiful," he remarked.

"Thank you. Everything up here is beautiful."

"That it is," he responded as he walked up the back steps.

He was now within feet of her. She smelled inviting. Poison he thought. Her golden locks draped on her silk covered shoulders. He quickly glanced at her cleavage covered by the bright silken blouse. He then gazed directly at her very blue eyes and she directly into his. They connected meaningfully and then she said, "Minute Maid or Tropicana?"

"Minute Maid," he responded, grabbed the wet glass, drank a gulp and commented, "Now, that hits the spot."

She glanced at him over one shoulder, sensually as she turned to grab a glass of juice for herself. "I think I will join you."

For a quick few seconds, his mind quietly envisioned them in a big Jacuzzi filled with orange juice and champagne. Wouldn't that be captivating!

"So are you settling in?" she inquired.

"Yes. How long have you lived here?"

"About five years."

"I bet you love every minute here."

"That I do. As you can understand, it is quite relaxing. A great place for beauty and reflection."

"How much time do you actually spend here?" he inquired.

"I try to spend up to two months, if possible. At least a month in the summer, maybe the first two weeks in July, two to four weeks in August including the week of the Gerald Ford tournament. And then scattered weeks, mostly during the winter months. Christmas, New Year's and other scattered times," she said.

"What brought you here from Vancouver? And why not property at Whistler Mountain; isn't that supposed to be the number one ski resort?"

"Well number one or two to Vail, depending on the ski magazine you read. I don't know. I actually live at the base of Whistler Mountain and do ski there as well. But I have always loved Colorado. Aspen. Telluride. And here. This is pleasant. And it is a family spot. Not all the glitz of Aspen, Telluride or Whistler. I like that down-to-earth feeling."

"Like Midwest values."

"What's that?"

"Midwest values represent the down-to-earth people, the farmers, the good and decent hard working middle class of the Midwest states, Iowa, Nebraska, Kansas, Minnesota, Illinois, Indiana, you know near Lake Michigan where the winds howl, the snows fall, and people spend a lot of time indoors with their families. Do you have a family Bailey?"

"Actually my mother and father live in San Francisco. My four brothers live in various places. Seattle, Carmel, New York and here in Denver."

"Are any of them cardiologists?"

"My father was a banker, taught Finance at UCal Berkeley and my mother was an artist. My brother in Seattle is a successful accountant, my brother in Carmel practices psychiatry, my brother in New York is an attorney, and my brother in Denver is a businessman with some real estate interests. He was the one who sold me on Arrowhead."

"Is that right?"

"Yes, he thought it was going to be a top real estate investment as well as a great place to live and he's been right. It's beautiful as you can see, and is appreciating in value."

"Yes, it is quite lovely. Even if it doesn't make money. How do you afford two months away from your cardiology practice back in Vancouver?"

"Actually I am on the faculty there at the University and quite involved in research with a part time practice. So I manage my time quite well, maximizing leisure where I can."

"I should say," said Robert, in his own mind, favorably applauding this bright attractive cardiologist for her time efficiency. "What is your subspecialty or interest area?"

"Nuclear cardiology with an interest in the neurosciences."

"A booming area, with remarkable research taking place."

"How about yourself, Robert, as I recall you were a well known echo cardiologist with Doppler expertise."

"That's correct. Your memory serves you well. Were you aware of my work before?"

"As I indicated I had an echo cardiographer friend and we went to your interesting panel with David Tipp of Stanford and Rudy Amonno of Kentucky, or was it California?"

"Well Rudy was in California, but is now at Kentucky. That was a fun panel. This is fun to be with you, but Danielle is waiting for me for breakfast. Bailey, thanks for the orange juice. It was terrific."

"Stop by again. I'll be glad to nourish your body and share some conversation."

Robert looked at her and thought I bet you would and so would I. "Well, thanks again."

"Robert would you care to play golf this afternoon? I have a threesome and would welcome you as the fourth."

"Well, thanks. Let me think about it. How soon do I have to get back to you?"

"I'll leave it open for you."

"Great. I'll let you know in the next hour or two," Robert replied. Well this will be an interesting conversation with Danielle he thought as he walked back on the path toward his town home. Imagine how my learning in cardiology would be accelerated if I had daily conversations with Bailey. We probably wouldn't have a tough time holding a conversation. But as he reflected on it, Danielle and he never were at a lost for words. In fact they even enjoyed the quiet times together. Could probably enjoy quiet times with Bailey as well, he mused.

Stepping lively into the townhouse Robert quickly remarked, "It is absolutely beautiful here in the morning, Danielle."

"I thought you got lost," she retorted.

"No such luck," he joked back. "What's for breakfast?"

"I made some scrambled eggs with eggbeaters, fruit and those bagels we picked up yesterday in Frisco."

"Great. I need some nourishment to accelerate my life-long learning."

"Lifelong learning acceleration. I love it," she responded. "What made you think of lifelong learning?"

"Well, remember yesterday when we were talking about how long we would live?"

"Yes."

"Well, I was thinking about it overnight. Like you I want to live to be one hundred and twenty. Just to see how stimulating the conversation will be in our one hundreds."

"I hear you. You have doubts that it will be stimulating then?"

"Not really. It is just interesting to try to speculate about the content of those conversations sixty and seventy years from now and with whom."

"With whom? You don't think I will be an active participant in those conversations then?"

"Oh sure. But I was wondering who else might participate among our children, grandchildren, great grandchildren. Goodness can you imagine the discussions on cardiology then? We will probably be in nuclear laboratories surrounded with millions of microscopic data too complex to decipher with computer/TV/telephone/electronic fiber optics analyzing our conversations in thousands of ways. It will be wild."

"At that point I will be in the backyard here doing my Grandma, or should I say Great Grandma Moses artist drawings of these beautiful mountains. I will leave the complex overloaded cardiology data for you to analyze. Give me the simple sunny days on this Colorado slope."

"But seriously, Danielle. We have talked about being lifelong learners for decades. And remember your friendly President, Diane Jackson, highlighted the concept in her first campaign and first book. How are you revising your lifelong learner plan?"

"That is what I hope to refine this week or next."

"Well in my remaining seventy five years I see at least five phases," Robert chimed in. "The next fifteen are real clear, dedicated to cardiology research and teaching pursuits. The class we have coming into the University this year will be the most diversified ever. Of the eighty students coming in we have twenty six countries represented. It is almost fifty-fifty female to male. That is unheard of in cardiology programs. Can you imagine the diversified research base we will have expanding in those twenty-six countries? Those students stretch the number of countries we have represented in the past ten years from fifty-two to sixty-seven countries, including China, Zimbabwe and Russia. I have a sense that sometime in this coming decade I will pursue some brain research, connect it to my heart research and perhaps explore the origins of the emotions and ordo amoris."

"Will you still be at Georgetown, here in Colorado, or somewhere else, say Canada?"

"I don't know," said Robert, stopped in his tracks by Danielle's question. Why did she say Canada? And why is she still hung up on living in Colorado? Is she trying to trump me up or get my goat? "How about you, Mother Teresa, or Grandma Moses where and what will you do in the coming decade or two?"

"Well, I am sure parenting will occupy a good portion of my learning as well as be fulfilling."

"So, you think you are pregnant?"

"Chance. But if not now, probably soon, wouldn't you concur?"

"I would concur."

"Do you think I or we will have to learn a lot on raising children appropriately?"

"Appropriately? I think I will just follow my heart and intuition," he said.

Danielle laughed. "Sure. You of all people. Mr. Doctor of Logic and Science. Dr. Seuss, Dr. Spock here I come. Who are you kidding? You're all heart and intuition."

"It landed me you, and we have done okay for eight years."

"You don't really believe it is only because you followed your heart and intuition?"

"Well then what was it?"

"A well-crafted personal and professional lifelong learning plan encompassing Stephen Covey's seven principles multiplied with an X-factor, diagnosed with a microscope and submitted to the Pope and Chancellor of the University for review and comment."

"Very original, Danielle. Obviously my continuing review and revision of the original or modified plan since I was seventeen has contributed greatly over these past twenty-eight years. Plus your special counsel, insight and suggestions over the same period of time."

"What significant suggestions of mine have you adopted in the past two years?"

"Better exercise and diet habits. It is only the Häagen-Dazs I miss the most, and the scientific data is inconclusive."

"Very funny. But I must admit when you were age forty-three, I thought that your extra twenty pounds cramped your mental and physical prowess, so you have made significant progress over the past two years. Thank you. You are to be applauded."

"How about for you, Danielle. What did you change and what did I contribute to your individual self-learning plan, personal and professional?"

Stumped initially, Danielle said, "I would have to think about that." She was stalling. In fact she was thinking of the significant impact William Hart had on her in that same time period. She was having trouble focusing on Robert. "You were there for me. Listening and understanding as you do. You are a good facilitator and probably could make a living as a professional facilitator in board rooms, corporate or university, or for that matter," reflecting on her own sex, "probably be quite effective with women's groups, professional or social."

"I have learned over the years the value of active listening with my students, my research, faculty members, and you, Danielle, you are a good listener. You have a very keen sense of both verbal and non-verbal cues. And you let others complete their own sentences and thoughts before you comment. That is a gift. In Washington, D.C. no one is allowed to complete their sentences or thoughts."

"Unless it is in a Senate filibuster," she commented.

"And then they let them go on for hours and days, don't they?"

"Likely. It is one of the more arcane rules that we need to dispense with," Danielle added. Returning to Robert's comment, "You are an excellent listener, Robert. Did you primarily learn that with your ear for music and the piano?"

"I think that music helped... to hear sounds emerging, to hear the unsaid, the unsung, the note about to be played, yes, definitely."

"It is remarkable Robert, your extraordinary talent as a pianist as well as a cardiologist."

"There are a number of cardiologists who are talented in music. From those playing with the Preservation Hall Jazz Band to the leading symphony orchestras in our country. But how about you, Danielle? How do you see your life in the coming decades?"

"You mean in addition to the decade or two of parenting?"

"Exactly. Knowing you, you will have multiple interests. You always have, always do, and always will."

"I think I will always be involved in the creative human causes. Most of them, such as in the past few years will involve children and women. At times, I toy with the freedom of independence, of doing some type of art, be it drawing, music or the fine arts. You know, put my Masters in Fine Arts to good use. To further develop some thought of my most stimulating mentors. Some creative and expressive thought. The arts are such an inspiration for humankind. I don't think we appreciate them enough. I know they don't in Washington, D.C. even though you and I know many creative people and there are many cultural outlets. I mean the people there are probably the brightest in the world. I am sure those in New York, San Francisco, perhaps London, Paris, Vienna or Hong Kong might disagree."

"Or Santa Fe, Chicago, Atlanta, Montreal, Quebec or Singapore."

"But I often think, Robert, that the fine arts might be pursuits better left to my late years. For the next several decades, I'll stick to social agendas. Often when I get in a free and open atmosphere like this, my mind quite naturally drifts to the creative arts. Flowers, mountains, large bodies of water, beautiful sunrises and sunsets, stimulate one beyond the everyday bustle of Washington, D.C."

"That is what vacations are for, refreshing and reviving one's spirit. Getting in touch with ourselves and having the time to relax and reflect on one's priorities and core values."

"I agree. I feel so fortunate to have so many professional options," Danielle said.

"And personal options as well."

"And personal options. Choices and roles as well, like where and when to have a baby."

"And with whom," Robert exclaimed.

"And with whom," Danielle smilingly agreed. Yet she was thinking how funny that Robert would say that. She was thinking of William as well as Robert as potential fathers. Although it appeared Robert might have gotten the early lead based on the communion here in the mountains. It was as lovely a lovemaking as she had enjoyed in her life.

"Danielle, how will having children affect what you are doing in Washington, D.C.?"

"Well it would obviously change my daily routine. I guess I would have to see how I was feeling. Right now, I see myself working as long as possible, right up to the delivery. Then I would take off four to six weeks with the baby, and return to work part-time after that."

"And knowing your present schedule, that would mean cutting your hours from eighty hours a week down to forty."

"That's a pretty good estimate. I always want to feel that I am helping more people than just myself and my family. Obviously I would be there for my baby. Even if, God forbid, something tragically happened to you, I would be there helping you however I could."

"And similarly I would be there for you Danielle."

All of a sudden Danielle imagined both Robert and William becoming more dependent on her. She felt afraid that both would require her personal care at the same time. My God, she thought, that would be a challenge, with or without a baby. Her sisters, mother and girlfriends, would help with the children. Danielle thought of William and how alone he must be even though he has children and constituents. William was more alone than Robert. But why? He was a very public man, accomplished, with family and friends. Why would she perceive him to be more alone than Robert? Maybe because Danielle had met Robert's family, friends, and colleagues. Danielle did not know those close to William except for some of his staff.

"Danielle?"

"Yes," she responded, a bit startled.

"What were you thinking? You seem to have drifted."

"A bit," she responded, trying to re-establish her focus.

"Maybe two bits."

"I was trying to imagine how I would juggle children and my profession."

"And?"

"And, it would be quite a change. And I guess that is why we marry, for better or for worse."

"And, being spoiled as we are, we always assume, quite naturally, that it is for the better. Why focus on the worse? Unless of course, you are Mother Teresa, as some call you, and you are there to respond to the needs of the world."

"Well I don't know about the needs of the world. At the present time, I am quite appreciative that I am here with you, in this beautiful house, this beautiful valley. The sun is shining. We have eaten well. We have an open day. And we have each other."

"You hit it on the head. We have had very rewarding lives, personally and professionally. We have more than most people can probably dream of. Yet we are still faced with the human condition, and its millions and trillions of options, and can spend time reflecting on it and making it even better."

For a solid moment they sat at the table, and smiled, looking longingly and thankfully at each other. They then slowly moved toward each other and connected their warm lips in an invigorating kiss.

As they parted, Danielle was the first to break the silence. "So Robert, what do you want to do? Play a round of golf here at Arrowhead, I suspect."

Of course she was right. "That is a distinct possibility.

Did you feel like playing?" he asked, wanting instead to join Bailey's group.

"I don't know. I am enjoying just being here. I could sit outside and read or write on our deck or at the pool," she said. "Would you like to do that Robert, or do you prefer to golf?"

He contemplated the options. Robert felt like playing golf. But how to tell Danielle. He thought about telling Danielle he would just walk over to the club with his golf clubs and join a foursome. But what if Danielle wanted to accompany him to the club on her way to the pool? Perhaps he could convince Danielle to reflect on her self-learning plan on the deck out back while the thoughts were still fresh in her mind.

"Well, Robert?"

"Well, if I play golf, you could work on your self-learning plan," he stated. "You seemed to enjoy our discussion this morning, and this setting will inspire you."

"Yes," she responded, seriously thinking again of William and how William would probably enjoy sitting with Danielle on the deck or at the pool. This was crazy, she thought, all the preoccupation with William. Was it because she and Robert had enjoyed satisfying sex, that she now yearned for William? Why this preoccupation with both men? And why wasn't she satisfied with Robert? He was loved by all. She laughed to herself, William and Robert both could win elections, but Danielle had to admit to herself that Robert would probably get more votes than William. Robert had never been tested politically and didn't have the enemies William had.

"Robert, why don't you go play your golf. I will have a fulfilling day regardless of what I do out here."

"Okay, I think I'll get ready then. I may make a call over to the club," he stated, knowing that he needed to call Bailey. He could make that call from their bedroom upstairs while Danielle was downstairs.

"Hello, Bailey. Yes I would love to play golf with you and your friends today. Good. I will see you at the club in about an hour," said Robert and then he hung up the phone and began to get ready.

Danielle wandered upstairs a short while later. "Well, did you get a golf game together? Who you are playing with?"

"Actually, I called Dr. Bailey Trudeau up and she said they had a threesome set up and I could join them."

"Well, that's great," Danielle responded, a bit surprised that Robert had made such a bold and assertive move. Although Robert was known in some circles for his moderate approach to the practice of cardiology, Robert was quite likely to assert himself as a successful, self-confident person. Danielle would never forget how she was taken by Robert the first time she met him. As a self-assured and accomplished woman in Washington, D.C. she wasn't impressed by many men. As she thought about that, William and Barry were two of only a few others she really liked upon first meeting them.

"Are the other two individuals that are playing golf with you and Bailey cardiologists?" Danielle inquired.

"I don't know," said Robert. "Probably a fifty-fifty chance. What I'm sure of is that one or two are competitive golfers. As a matter of fact, I know that's the case from what Bailey said yesterday."

"Isn't it true of most cardiologists you play golf with?" Danielle remarked.

"As a matter of historic fact, you are right again Danielle." It was amazing how Danielle and Robert could read each other. They were married eight years now, but it was still uncanny how either might finish the other's thought pattern if given the opportunity. They made a great team of intellectual and psychic insight.

"Have you decided what you will do?" Robert inquired.

"Perhaps I will start with an interesting walk as you did this morning," said Danielle, cutting to the core reality of the situation, even though it appeared she was not aware of Robert's and Bailey's meeting this morning.

"I am sure it will lead you to a most rewarding morning and afternoon of delights," Robert said.

"Yes, it will," stated Danielle as she prepared to show her well trimmed body in a skin clinging silver and pink running outfit with a beautiful pink bow surrounding her closely cropped pony tail. She would enjoy her afternoon of freedom.

Chapter Seven
Love

On the practice green, Bailey brought over her two playing partners to meet Robert. The couple, seemingly out of a Hollywood movie, with golden bronze tans and great looking physiques, were introduced as Don Jacobson and Kerry Landreau. Don looked like a former quarterback who Robert hadn't seen since his college days at Illinois. Robert initially speculated that Don was in his late thirties. Bailey said, "Robert is a leading international cardiologist from Georgetown University in Washington, D.C."

"Washington, D.C. is one of my favorite cities," Kerry exclaimed. "And Georgetown has a great reputation. You may have heard of my father, Jacques Landreau; he used to be a visiting professor there."

"I do know Jacques. From his research of course. You are not a cardiologist, are you Kerry?" Robert inquired.

"No. I am a psychiatrist from Santa Barbara actually. But I deal with a lot of hearts."

"Yes, I bet you do," Robert replied.

"And Don is in real estate development in Lake Tahoe," Bailey said.

"How come you are slumming here in Colorado? Do you have real estate interests here as well?" Robert asked.

"Actually I do. I built Bailey's home, and I have a few other friends here in Arrowhead and Beaver Creek. But I am based out of Lake Tahoe."

"A beautiful place," Robert offered.

"You have been there, I presume," replied Don.

"Yes, a good friend of mine retired there and is a writer

128

now. He used to be a practicing cardiologist, a good one."

"Well, Robert, so much for introductions. Don is a four handicap and Kerry is a nine handicap. How about you and I playing them and we will get two shots a side on the two toughest handicap holes on each side."

"Bailey you are the gambler. I am not sure I will play to my ten handicap on a challenging foreign course," Robert stated.

"Well maybe you need to give us the shots because this foreign country you are talking about is Vail, Colorado, where your ball will go miles. And besides, you are probably a big hitter," Kerry responded looking interestingly at Robert's athletic physique.

"Well we can always readjust at nine if it is way out of line," Don chimed in, knowing he was a solid four handicap who had shot seventy-six and seventy-seven the two prior days.

"Kerry, your honors, off of your great eighty two days ago," Bailey said.

"How many shots are we getting, Bailey?" Robert inquired amusingly, but thinking he and Bailey would be in for a tough game.

"Now, now, not to worry," said Bailey as she approached the tee box and watched Kerry's initial drive go over two hundred yards down the center of the fairway. Bailey proceeded to hit it almost as far, again straight down the middle of the fairway.

Watching those two impressive drivers, Robert said, "Would one of you want to hit my drive as well?"

"I am sure you can top both of those," said Kerry, ever the confident golden girl athlete. She looked like a former combination beauty queen and golf star, like one or two model types from the pro golf ranks.

Robert turned to offer Don the first shot. "Don, you want

to show me the way."

"No, that's fine. You are the guest. Lead off."

It was a warm eighty degrees with a slight breeze from the North. Feeling some pressure yet thankful to be on the golf course, Robert teed up, viewed down the fairway and hit it about two hundred and forty yards. It was in the middle of the fairway, slightly ahead of both women's golf balls.

Don, the best handicap of the four, hit a beauty about two hundred and seventy yards in the fairway with a slight right to left hook on the ball.

"What an atrocious start," laughed Bailey, as all four walked down the fairway with their personal caddies.

The round was extremely satisfying on the front side. Robert participated in the small talk on each hole. The foursome were good conversationalists. Don was relaxed and the best golfer, shooting thirty-eight on the front side, only two over par. That was equal his handicap. Kerry shot forty, one better than her handicap and Bailey shot forty-one, only one over her handicap. Robert came in with a forty-two, only slightly off his handicap. Robert and Bailey were two down at the turn, not bad considering Don and Kerry were shooting so well.

"Well should we adjust the handicap or are two shots still good enough for the back nine?" offered Kerry, wanting to be fair, and as the psychiatrist, offering her crisp analysis.

Bailey and Robert turned to look at one another, not a bad view from either perspective. Playfully Bailey said, "Robert what do you think?"

Not knowing how the competition might end, but hopeful that he and Bailey might improve their game on the back side, Robert said, "Well I was thinking three or four shots."

Don was quick to pick up, "I was thinking of offering you

five to six shots." Bailey and Kerry both laughed simultaneously saying, "Sure, why not more?"

"Well give us one more shot and maybe it will be a tad closer on the return nine."

"Got it," Don said, knowing when to close a deal.

The back nine was equally enjoyable and intensely competitive. Robert noticed that when she could, Kerry asked him penetrating questions. He wondered if she was asking the questions for her own personal interest or Bailey's. Although he felt that they were her genuine personal interests, he didn't doubt for a minute that these two women would later exchange perspectives on their male golf partners. Seemingly, the women knew Don. At least Robert surmised that Kerry and Don may have been very close friends, although all three exchanged pleasantries and fun loving comments. It truly was an enjoyable round. Robert enjoyed the golf and the company.

Kerry was especially interested in knowing about Danielle, to Robert's amusement. All three were politically astute, not common in most doctors. Don's real estate and development work required him to have a solid background in the Washington scene, especially the work of the Senate Finance and House Ways and Means Committees. All three were intrigued when Robert shared with them Danielle's extensive government relations in Washington, D.C. including the White House.

"Robert, did you go to Washington thinking you would find a politically astute wife?" Kerry asked somewhat out of the blue.

He laughed and said, "Believe me, I never contemplated marriage as part of the Washington equation. I am sure as Bailey would attest, most of us cardiologists are pretty well preoccupied with our practice. For me, the priorities are research and continued learning, as well as practical contributions to the future of cardiology."

Bailey contributed, "Sometimes a marriage can limit the contributions one makes to cardiology."

"You mean like in your case?" Kerry responded. She and Don both laughed.

Robert was intrigued.

"Yes, definitely," Bailey responded with uncharacteristic severity.

Robert reflected on the comments.

"You see, Robert," Bailey said, "for three years I was married to Richard Trudeau." Robert recognized him as the leading Canadian cardiovascular surgeon, well known for his pioneering work in coronary bypass surgery and his peer-reviewed contributions, including several in the well-respected New England Journal of Medicine and the British journal, LANCET.

"That must have been an interesting time," Robert commented attempting to make light conversation, yet interested to see Bailey's as well as the others' response. Don and Kerry had their eyes glued on Bailey.

"Interesting it was," responded Bailey as she stepped up to the eighteenth tee after making a remarkable birdie on seventeen with a long putt. "What about double or nothing?" Bailey confidently stated, staking her claim as a risk taker and gambler. Robert, shunning aside any further commentary, was impressed with her confidence.

Kerry quickly responded on behalf of the leading twosome. Kerry and Don were still playing well. Robert was playing okay but he couldn't putt these mountain greens at Arrowhead. Bailey was on fire, one under for the last four holes and two over on the backside. The eighteenth hole was a challenging par four, with water and an elevated green. The green also had all types of undulations and was well known for the swing of many a match.

All four had great drives. Kerry shot first from the fairway and was the first to hit the green in regulation, but she was on the low side of the green, still having to putt up two elevations to the pin in the back of the green. Bailey hit next and was fortunate to get to the middle of the green at middle elevation. Robert followed and also reached the middle elevation, but his shot, a strong iron, bit up and came to rest a few feet in front of Bailey's ball. Don hit the best iron into the green and was the only one to hit on the top elevation, only eighteen feet from the pin. He had the best shot for a birdie and the match.

Kerry was first to putt. She needed to go up two elevations. It was a very tough putt. She hit it well enough to make the top elevations, but was still six to seven feet away from her par.

Bailey was next to putt. How she wanted this putt for a score of thirty-seven on the back side, her best ever and for the match. She stroked it firmly to the high side of the hole. It rimmed the cup.

Everyone simultaneously let out a loud "Ooohh."

Bailey's putt ended up three feet beyond the hole.

Robert was next to putt. His putt was twenty-four feet away with a winding left to right movement to the hole. He had learned the break from Bailey's ball, that had been only about ten feet behind him when she stroked it firmly. Robert felt confident and wanted it as Bailey wanted hers. Robert slowly brought his bull's eye putter back and evenly struck through the ball. The ball started its break along the path of destiny, breaking to the center of the cup.

Kerplunk! It went in!

"Just like TV," Bailey calmly and confidently stated.

"Yes," Robert exclaimed.

"Great putt," Kerry added.

"Yes, exceptional putt under pressure," Don offered, moving to line his eighteen foot putt up and hoping for the same result as Robert's. Calmly, assuredly, Don lined it up. He stroked it firmly towards the cup, but he rimmed it on the high side.

"No," he said closing his eyes and looking skyward.

"Great shot and great match," Kerry congratulated first Robert and then Bailey. She assuredly completed her round by knocking her three footer in after Kerry missed her six footer.

"Great round, Bailey," Kerry congratulated her. "Thirty-eight on the back side for seventy-nine. Robert you finished with eighty and Don you had thirty-nine for seventy-seven. I had eighty-one. That was fun."

"Yes, it was. Some great golf gang," Don said.

"Yes, thanks to all of you, I really enjoyed it," Robert added.

"Bailey, thanks a million. I really enjoyed it. Congratulations for a great backside."

"Well, thank you, pros. It was great to have your closing birdie to even things up here on eighteen," Bailey reached out and firmly shook Robert's hand, while placing her left hand on his forearm.

Robert grasped Bailey's strong hand and simultaneously put his left arm on her forearm. Then surprisingly, Bailey kissed Robert on his cheek, whispering in his ear, "Thanks, sport."

"You're welcome," Robert returned, feeling an extra special thank you from his new-found cardiologist friend.

"Bailey shall we all have a drink up on the deck and replay

the round?" Kerry asked.

"Will you join us, Robert, for a drink?"

"Sure, I'll have one," he said knowing that a great round of golf was completed with three beautiful people, two he wouldn't mind continuing conversation with. But he quickly thought of Danielle, wondering what she had done this afternoon and whether she was waiting for him or preoccupied with something else.

"Well, Doctor Anderson, you can handle my heart troubles anytime," Kerry said. "The way you responded with that putter on eighteen, I wouldn't mind having you as my playing partner next time," she added, looking coyly over to Don as she finished her comment.

"Yeah, I wouldn't mind teaming up with you as well," Don responded. "It would be interesting to see how the gals would pair up against us," he added.

"Either way," Robert said, keeping his options open. "But Bailey and I wouldn't mind playing with you on a rematch either," he blinked over to her.

"Yeah, we'll give you a rematch next time. But the stakes will be higher," Bailey said.

Don asked, "What were we playing for anyway?"

"Pride and some Dom Perignon," Bailey quickly added.

"And the dinner," Kerry continued. "Which by the way Robert, will you and Danielle join us for dinner tonight here at the Bristol?"

Hesitating, but knowing he would enjoy it as would Danielle, Robert responded, "Can I let you know, Bailey?" turning her way. "I would like to see what Danielle might have in mind."

"Sure, you can call me at home and let us know. We would love to have you join us for dinner."

***

After conferring with Danielle, Robert called Bailey and said they would join them at the Bristol at seven thirty that evening.

The sun began its glorious descent in the west, revealing a rainbow of colors in the sky and on the mountains. Robert and Danielle walked west from their town home, up a small incline to the club and its five star restaurant, where Bailey, Kerry and Don waited at the entrance.

As Danielle and Robert approached, all the women eyed each other. Bailey was the first to greet Danielle, "Danielle great to see you again. I would like you to meet my friends, Kerry and Don."

"Great to meet you all," she responded. "Robert said it was a touch of heaven out there today with the three of you."

Kerry kicked in, "He didn't tell you that there might be a fallen angel or two amidst the crowd."

"You did say your name was Kerry," Danielle quickly came back.

All five laughed.

"Well, we could call Lucifer to make it an even six," Robert chimed in.

"Here's a phone, I'll call him," Don said. All laughed again.

"Yes it was heavenly," Bailey approvingly commented. "Especially when the twenty-four footer dropped on eighteen."

"Okay, so some of us are poor putters and like to contribute to others' well-being," Kerry added.

"Precisely," added Don.

"Robert says you enjoy the game as well, Danielle,"

Bailey said as they sat down.

"Yes, but not at the same skill level as all of you."

"Robert told us of your exceptional skill in Washington however," Kerry said.

"He did, did he? What insightful commentary did he provide?"

Kerry continued, "He says you are a seasoned government relations professional, equally adept on the Hill or in the White House."

"Yes, it has been fun applying one's sense of love, fairness and justice to the process."

"Well, that is a different perspective of Washington, D.C. from the one we have on the West Coast," Kerry said.

"Oh, what is your perspective from California?"

"Robert already filled you in on our geographic preferences as well as politics?" Kerry asked.

"Well at least some of the geography. I am a little less clear on your political preferences," Danielle continued.

"Well I'm somewhere between Jack and Bobby Kennedy and our former governor Ronald Reagan. Bailey preferred Jefferson and Aaron Burr. Don is a cross between Pat Buchanan, Steve Forbes and Attila the Hun," Kerry said.

The group had a good laugh.

"Well, coming from Washington, D.C. I am quite familiar with Attila the Hun. Except we called him Mr. Speaker."

The group laughed again.

"The reason Kerry loved Jack and Bobby Kennedy is that she never escaped the Irish ghetto, and was it you Kerry or your mother who was their West Coast psychiatrist?" Bailey responded.

"It was my father, Jimmy Hoffa, who shot pool with them," Kerry commented.

"Yes and then played cards all night," Don added.

The group laughed again. They ordered some California wine and continued the banter.

"Well I can see this conversation will be as dull as those in Congressional receptions," Danielle said.

"Do you enjoy those, Danielle?" Kerry inquired.

"Well they are real love fests, especially close to election time. But I prefer my love in more intimate settings."

"Love, now that will be a great theme for the evening. We probably all concur that it's the preferred emotion in intimate settings."

"Here, here," Don raised his wine glass.

"The vote is five to zero for the love theme."

"I'll abstain," Kerry humorously added.

"From the vote or the wine?" Bailey asked.

"The vote, of course. I never fully appreciate why people abstain from voting unless there is a conflict of interest. I fully believe, like the majority of you cardiologists, that life and the heart have ordo amoris. And all of us have preferences, leanings of love I call them."

"I love that, leanings of love, it should be a book title," Danielle contributed.

"And a movie," Don added.

"Don't you cardiologists think that there are strong poles of positive and negative powers in our life, emanating from the heart and predisposing most action on earth?" Kerry asked.

Bailey and Robert deferred to one another. Bailey was the first to speak. "Yes, I believe, and I think we need to underline believe, because I see belief as the baseline for any human action. Do you believe love is compassionate and nurturing?"

Before Bailey would conclude her insights, Danielle was

feeling the same thoughts, ideas, words and beliefs. "That is exactly as I view it. Fundamentally, we believe in being lovers, nurturers, helpers, servants, compassionate human beings who truly love one another and want to help, serve and love one another."

Robert said, "I see it, think it and understand it similarly. Love is celebration of life. It is like this meal after a wonderful day of golf. And it is not just because I won today, although I am sure that helps my feeling."

"It helps your feeling. Assuredly it does," Don interrupted.

"Okay it does help. But I am enjoying this meal and the company. We are fortunate to be blessed people, if I may so boldly state, with certain skills to help other people in medicine, politics and real estate."

"Well, you are kind," Don acknowledged.

Robert continued, "Love is the most important element in life. It allows us to share in the beauty and conscious celebration of every moment. It is what motivates us to help another person. The best kind of love is unconditional."

Danielle said, "I think you, Robert, and Bailey provided valuable insight into the properties of love. To me it encompasses the great virtues, principles and commandments of life. Like responsibility, truthfulness, fairness, respect for life, freedom, tolerance and the kind of unity we feel here and now. And, you don't have to be at the Bristol in Arrowhead to feel it."

"But it doesn't hurt," Don said.

"No it doesn't hurt, but each of us has felt love in many different places and in different ways. We will be fortunate to experience it again," Kerry said.

"Since our arrival to Arrowhead, Robert and I have been discussing lifelong learning plans as well as our love. We have concluded that we are taking it for granted or making assumptions rather than trying to analyze our love and applying it as the operating principle. We were thinking about having a baby. Do any of you have children?"

"I have an adopted boy," said Don.

"I have a boy and girl, fourteen and sixteen," said Kerry.

Robert looked surprised by Danielle's mention of children.

"I am thinking of adopting a two year old Chinese boy," added Bailey.

"How wonderful for all three of you," Danielle commented.

"I think it is great that you want to be parents. You will find it very rewarding. Truly an inspiration of love. Oh, believe me, you will have times when parenting appears to be the farthest thing from love. But it is those poles of life, those extremes of love, warm love and tough love that are most meaningful."

"Well, Kerry is talking about those teenage years, but we can all remember how challenging those years were for us as teenagers," Bailey interrupted.

"Yes, I remember how far away I was from pre-medicine. Basketball and football were king," said Robert.

"Trying to compete for the attention of boys, teachers, coaches and whoever else," said Kerry.

"Yeah, but Kerry, not all were Olympic-bound like you were. Your father was Chancellor of the University and your mother was curator of one of the finest museums in the Southwest," Bailey added.

"True," Kerry acknowledged.

"Love is always tougher when you have such crosses," Don offered.

"Is it?" Danielle responded.

"Yes, is it?" Bailey also questioned. It seemed to Robert that Bailey and Danielle were often on the very same train of thought. It was eerie how they could pick up each other's thoughts and complete them. He listened keenly to their comments and to those of Kerry hoping to identify the strong similarities in their thinking.

"Well, I know I felt loved by my parents, but they also expected much from me because they were successful. You have heard it said that success often breeds success. Well my parents' successes were an inspiration. They were role models for me and my siblings. We were most fortunate to have their example. There are so many young people who don't have parents or other mentors who take a genuine interest in them and genuinely love them. I am amazed how many people have children, yet lack the necessary information on both the responsibilities and the joys of raising them. That is the key to their success later on in life," said Kerry.

"Amen," the group reiterated.

"What you shared is very true, Kerry. As Robert and I have shared many times, our parents' unconditional love for us was the main factor in developing happy and successful lives. Happiness and success may be defined in various ways, but love penetrates all of it. I think nurturer rings closest to love for me. Who nurtures who and how. Parents nurture their children. A man and wife nurture each other just like any two human beings, be they male or female, nurture each other in a loving friendship or relationship."

"Danielle and I have often reflected on the nurturing aspect of any loving relationship. If we focus on the help and service we provide, we will clearly love each other with all our heart and soul. Erich Fromm, the world famous psychologist, described people as starved for love, which he defined as 'an art requiring knowledge and effort,'" said Robert.

"He also emphasized humility, courage, discipline and faith as critical to that act of love," Kerry responded.

"My mother used to say love was being fulfilled in others," Bailey said.

"It is the ultimate support provided to others," Don added.

"I like to think love draws people in. Loving someone enriches them because you believe fully in their worth. And you enrich yourself in the process because you have connected as human beings and helped one another. This meal has a spiritual dimension. It is like a benediction and communion all in one. Makes you want to say hallelujah, doesn't it?"

"Hallelujah, Hallelujah," Danielle and Bailey said in unison.

The boys nodded in agreement as smiles shined on the entire party of five.

"Love is the most powerful influence in our lives," Bailey stated.

"We are very fortunate to share such a deep discussion among five bright and successful people who obviously grasp life's true blessing, and share in love," Danielle said.

"Makes you want to hug and kiss one another," Kerry said.

"Well maybe we can at least join hands so as not to create a scene in this restaurant," Bailey suggested.

They all looked at each other, and quietly held hands in a warm and fitting circle around the table. "Okay, now that we have had a wonderful golf day here at the Country Club of the Rockies, let's dance the night away at Club Chelsea," Kerry concluded.

Chapter Eight
Flow

Two weeks ended quickly for Danielle and Robert. Robert was able to golf often, most of the time with Bailey, with whom he had become quite close, and a few other times with Kerry and Don. Kerry and Robert also enjoyed a couple of rounds together. Danielle had done much deep introspection, and was quite open to having a baby now. She wasn't sure if she was pregnant, although she half-suspected that she was. She did quite a bit of cooking for Robert and herself. Bailey, Kerry and Don visited one night. Another evening, Danielle and Robert had dinner with Bailey. Bailey truly was an exceptional woman, Danielle thought. It was quite obvious that she and Robert had much in common, both professionally and personally. Danielle thought that they mentally respected each other's knowledge base and proficiency regarding cardiology. She was somewhat oblivious to Bailey's high regard for Robert's prominent position in cardiology. Danielle and Bailey seemed to get along quite famously, as if they were sisters or lifelong friends. Danielle was conscious of this closeness, as was Bailey. Robert also recognized their compatibility. All three had developed a remarkable interaction in such a short time period.

Danielle and Robert talked about the remarkable flow they experienced in their daily life together while in Arrowhead. In part, this was due to the fact that Danielle and Robert spent much more time together here than in Washington, D.C.

"Robert wouldn't you like to duplicate this flow in D.C.?"

"Yes, we have really enjoyed it haven't we?"

"As much as any two week time period in our lives together."

143

"Yes we have really delighted in the small and simple pleasures. Whether it was breakfast, lunch and dinner, or the walks in the morning or late at night," Robert said.

"Or your golf games with Bailey, Kerry, Don, and others."

"Or your cooking, reading, writing and reflecting."

"Obviously the setting contributed immensely," Danielle stated.

"I know, you want me to agree to set up a cardiology practice in the Vail Valley," Robert turned to look at Danielle.

"I didn't say that. It just flew from your tongue and heart and soul as you have come to contemplate it yourself," said Danielle.

"Well it is possible," acknowledged Robert.

"It is amazing how much more attentive you have become here, Robert, do you realize that?"

"Of course, I realized how focused I became on my golf game, steadily shooting in the high seventies and low eighties no matter what the pin placement on the course."

"And successful, whether it was in that initial golf match with Bailey and her friends or the other golf games you had the last two weeks."

"But it was more than the golf. I felt like I was more attentive to you and more focused on your present and future needs."

"That you were, Robert. And I felt the same way. I also felt you were quite open and receptive to others. Not that you usually aren't. I sensed you developed unique and strong relationships especially with Bailey and Kerry."

"Yes, they are interesting and fine people, and I did enjoy their company."

"You and I have made acquaintance with less attractive,

less bright and less loving people in Washington," added Danielle.

"Well speak for yourself, Danielle. I have enjoyed most everyone I have met, but I know less politicians than you do."

"Not all of my focus in Washington, D.C. is on politicians."

"I am aware of that Danielle, but the attention and focus that we have found here in Colorado is miles higher and deeper than the average relationship back in Washington."

"Well it is not because people in Washington aren't goal-oriented."

"Well, I wonder. The goals of people here focus upon a simple connectedness with one another and with nature."

"Maybe nature and the environment influences people. It is truly beautiful out here with the mountains, the sun rising and falling so gloriously on the mountaintops. The lush greenness of the grass and fairways and meadows. The breathtaking views from the valley."

"Could be the natural surroundings and beautiful environment. We do have the Potomac River back in Washington, D.C. And there is visible green grass on the ground. But very few people we encounter in a typical day back home take time to enjoy the Potomac River or green grass," Robert added.

"No they are focused on themselves."

"Yes, they are. We probably take ourselves much too seriously back in Washington, D.C. Not that this is necessarily all bad," said Robert.

"You know, when I think of our commitment, our involvement back in Washington, D.C. I think it is quite genuine, quite intense. Mine is for the women, children, and other vulnerable people who need and deserve better health care. And I know your commitment to your patients, colleagues and students is most genuine. Your cardiology pursuits could take place anywhere. Mine necessarily must be in Washington, D.C. But I don't believe others outside the Washington beltway believe we have that genuine involvement, or dedication. They don't believe that kind of genuine commitment is possible there. Do you think Bailey, Kerry and Don believed we are truly dedicated back East?" Danielle inquired.

"Why even ask such a thing? Yes I think they do even if at times they may have joked about it. Don and Kerry did kid about it, but in a friendly kind of way. Bailey may have been more understanding and compassionate."

"You really liked Bailey didn't you, Robert?"

"Yes, she's a fine person and I sense a very good cardiologist," he clarified. "As I think about all five of us, I think we are fortunate to have a positive flow to our lives. That discussion regarding children was quite insightful. Each of our lives has been quite rewarding and creative in many ways."

"Yes, I sensed a very high consciousness of life, and its values. It seemed that our consciousness individually and collectively was really flowing when we were engaged together in conversation, as we shared many deep and extensive insights about the real meaning of life and our priorities, individually and as a community. The real great and precious values of life," said Danielle.

"Yes, I sensed tremendous understanding. Although we were each distinct individuals, we also shared values, such as our personal and professional accomplishments and the belief that there was much more to experience and to contribute."

"Yes, you know Robert, despite the cat-and-mouse tonality of our conversations, I felt a penetrating trust, a love, a bind among us. We three women, all somewhat accomplished in our professional lives, had a genuine respect for each other. At the same time, there was a tension among us, which is to be expected when women are in the presence of two accomplished men."

Robert laughed. "The same trust and respect existed between Don and I. Although we were also somewhat competitive in our attempt to appeal to each of you striking women. That's the beauty of our sexes and our lives."

"Despite the competition, we collaborated in an interesting conversation about the possibilities and choices in our lives," said Danielle. "That flow among us was the beauty of the moment. We don't experience that flow of conversation enough. The synergy in that flow is the real essence of life. The setting was relaxed, in exact contrast to our demanding professional lives."

"But let's recognize the value of those professional experiences for all five of us, which involve human beings and fulfilling creative opportunities," remarked Robert.

"You are absolutely right about that. We need to clarify the creative possibilities more often, and initiate those opportunities to help the people we encounter each day. Help them to clarify their own goals and to realize greater personal and community fulfillment."

"Danielle, don't you think a major issue is that we don't actively listen to one another or provide constructive feedback. If we did this, we would feel greater control in our own lives and thus be more able to give back."

"That is true for many women, especially single ones, who need positive reinforcement from both women and men. One of my major concerns is the number of children, especially with single parents, who are greatly lacking in receiving and learning to give positive feedback, especially when they do something right. We need to congratulate them, reward them, recognize them immediately after they create a positive act."

"Motivation is key. I think of those best able to recover from heart attacks or bypass surgery. The positive intense motivation, the positive reinforcement is so key to recovery. Strong spouses and positive family members are key in that supportive and creative recovery environment," said Robert, thinking of the many patients he helped back to more rewarding, fulfilling and productive lives.

"I find that motivation is very much related to the amount of control people feel they have in their lives. You and I have been quite fortunate in our lives to have had great parents, as well as learning and growing environments growing up. We had strong support systems and strong role models. We were taught self-esteem regarding our potential, our abilities, our accomplishments. For us motivation was intrinsic. That isn't true in so many people we know. Think about it."

"You are right. Many of my heart patients obviously had low esteem which contributed to their heart attack. Poor diet and nutrition, lack of appropriate and timely exercise, extreme stress and the lack of needed assistance reflect a lack of self-esteem."

"And think of their recovery pattern and how their level of self-esteem contributed to that," added Danielle.

"You are right. I can think of numerous examples, hundreds of examples."

"Isn't the key, Robert, how open we are to our true self. How sensitive we are to ourself and to those with whom we work, live and play?"

"Play is key," said Robert, thinking of all the play they were able to incorporate over these last two weeks. And how much they enjoyed one another and others. They were open and sensitive to one another, to others, to the beauty of the time, place and moment.

"Robert, we were quite fortunate to be self-renewed, intrinsically motivated through this two week vacation, to fully express ourselves to one another and to others. Robert, I love you."

"I love you. I love you very much," Robert responded. They embraced. He smelled her beautiful scent. Her skin was radiant, soft and very warm.

Danielle felt her husband's gentle strength. Was that the baby, their baby, she was feeling inside her as they embraced? She closed her eyes for a brief moment as their bodies pressed against one another. She felt love like never before.

* * * * *

It was Sunday and time to determine life's priorities. The roles, responsibilities and relationships of Danielle and Robert were now under review.

It was a little after 7:00 a.m. They had an excellent night's sleep just like every other night over the past two weeks.

After breakfast they completed their packing to catch the 12:25 p.m. flight on United from Denver International Airport back to Washington Dulles.

Robert said he was going for his last morning walk, an almost daily ritual these last two weeks.

Robert headed east as he had often done. He approached Bailey's home. It was too early for her to be on her back deck, so Robert went around the front and rang the doorbell. He waited anxiously to say goodbye to his new friend and colleague.

Bailey opened the door dressed in a white elegant full-length robe.

"What a pleasant surprise," she said.

"Good morning."

Her robe slightly opened at her chest and thighs as she moved confidently toward Robert. "Would you like to come in?"

He paused, looking deliciously at the invitation before him and said, "Sure, why not."

She moved aside with her back to the door. She looked like an Amazon queen with her long flowing hair draped over her right shoulder and a confident stance. Once he stepped inside she boldly walked past him to her sunlit kitchen. She proceeded to the refrigerator to pour his favorite orange juice.

"Fabulous," he said, as he longingly downed the juice.

"Every healthy cardiologist needs plenty of vitamin C to get him going in the morning," Bailey responded as she drank her own healthy glass of juice.

"Well, Bailey, it has been a real pleasure to spend some quality time getting to know you," he remarked.

"Robert, I have enjoyed it immensely. Our golf games improved too."

"Yes, that is always a pleasure, especially when you play with competitive players."

"Competitive, yet positively refreshing in the process, more European or Caribbean than American maybe," she reflected.

"European or Caribbean than American?" he asked. He remembered the relaxed and enjoyable times he and Danielle had spent in France, Italy and the Caribbean.

"You know how it is on some relaxing European mountain or Caribbean setting," she said.

"Indeed, I do," he said as he sipped his juice. "Danielle and I are catching a 12:25 p.m. flight. I guess this means so long for a while."

"Oh," Bailey remarked, a bit startled, and wondering how to say goodbye to her new friend. She shifted to another part of the kitchen, to better glimpse his bronze face and body in the morning sunlight. "I am leaving later this afternoon after enjoying a few more hours of this glorious mountain sun and day," she added.

"Lucky you," he remarked sensing her anxiety.

"Robert, we are both lucky, to be here in this time and space, to have made our mutually rewarding acquaintance, and to be able to carry on, personally and professionally, maybe to eternity," she said boldly.

"Yes, we are and I look forward to our next encounter," he said.

"When and where do you think that might be?" she playfully inquired.

Never to be stumped for more than brief seconds, he retorted, "Maybe at the airport." He knew that wasn't likely, yet he was open to the possibility, as any good cardiologist could be in dealing with matters of the heart.

"What time and where shall we meet?" she gamed him as she sensually wound her fingers around the orange juice glass while tilting her head.

"How about three weeks in Hawaii at the East-West International Cardiology meeting?" he asked.

"What International Cardiology meeting?"

"I was kidding, but thought maybe we could at least have a panel discussion in the land of the rainbow," he returned.

"Very clever, doctor," she responded. "How about us doing it on Maui, that's my favorite island."

"Let me check my calendar and get back to you," he said, "sometime in the next few years."

She laughed. So did he. The game would go on. They really did enjoy each other's company.

"Are you going to the American Heart Association's Annual Meeting this year?" she asked.

"In San Francisco?"

"Yes."

"It's a possibility. I guess if I come out, I would like to tie in a few days in Monterey, Big Sur area," he said.

"One of my favorite haunts," she relayed. "So when do you start classes, next week or two?"

"Within two weeks. We have a great residents' class coming in this year," he said. "How about yourself, what does your upcoming week look like?"

"Actually I am trying to complete an article. We talked about it the other day."

"Yes, I think the subject area is badly in need of further exploration."

"Robert, there is a whole lot that deserves more exploration." She looked at him with a wrinkled brow.

"Yes, Bailey, you're right. Time and space exploration are an eternal quest." He smiled at her, finished his juice, and set down his glass on her counter top. As he turned around he found himself within two feet of this beautiful cardiologist. "I look forward to seeing you again Bailey."

"I look forward to seeing you, Robert." And with that brief comment, she softly kissed him directly on the lips.

His eyes open, he kissed her back. And that was that. They stood staring at each other. Reservedly longing, both realizing that they had come to a fork in the road and that they needed to choose a path. In some ways, both wanted the same path. At the same time, it was an encounter that would have to wait. For today, they would embark on separate yet connected journeys.

Ever playful, even for a straight A student, Bailey embraced and kissed him again passionately. He returned the feeling, yet knew it was time to go.

"See you, Bailey."

"See you, Robert."

He walked to the door, turned for a quick glance and smile, then left.

As he returned to the fresh morning air, he could see her face, feel her lips, and see her body within the elegant robe. At the same time he saw Danielle, clearing the breakfast table in the kitchen. He felt the best of both worlds, his independence and the independence of each woman. And yet, the bonds among them were strong. Such were the nuances of life. In one sense he didn't want to leave. In another sense he was glad to be on his way.

Danielle greeted him warmly as he entered the townhouse. "Did you have a good walk this morning?"

"Yes, it was quite invigorating. I will miss mornings in Colorado. The air is so fresh. The coolness of the morning puts one in touch with mother nature. The wetness on the grass and trees. The illuminating greens of the meadows. The beautiful clouds and morning sunrises. I love it here."

"Good enough to move here?"

"Almost good enough to move here. Leave your hot, political Washington for the fresh clear mountain air of Colorado. Why don't we just stay here, Danielle?"

Now he had her going. Just as she was packing up to leave.

"You couldn't be serious, Robert. Leave your Georgetown

faculty, friends and students?"

"Maybe I could ask the Dean to work something out. How about your caucus, Danielle, would they allow you to be based here? Less likely than the Georgetown faculty okaying my transcontinental arrangement I would bet."

"Maybe the caucus would get along just fine without me, Robert. We have developed some good leadership in just a short period of time."

"But the rest of Washington couldn't live without you. Especially your friends Cathryn, Gabriella and Susan. Not to mention the other women's groups, the Senators and Congressional representatives and their staffs."

As soon as Robert mentioned Senators, Danielle saw William in her mind. At once she became silent and reflective. Danielle started to reminisce about their times together including the recent lunch on the Hill and their get-together afterwards.

"Danielle, Danielle, did you hear me? You didn't respond."

"Yes, yes," she said, trying to get her composure back.

"You know," Danielle continued, "we really have had a terrific time here these two weeks. But I am ready to help my constituents get needed health reform. This significant change of pace sure has been invigorating. It has sensitized me to what is truly important. I appreciate our marriage, Robert. I appreciate your warmth and soothing friendship. Though our professional lives are different, they are entwined in the health arena. We are fortunate to be able to help other people in significant ways in our respective roles. For that I am grateful. For you I am grateful, Robert."

"Thank you, Danielle. I feel similarly grateful for you. And for us."

"And I am grateful for our weeks here, and our new friends, Bailey, Kerry and Don."

At the mention of Bailey, Robert returned to the kiss, fleeting yet powerful. Robert wondered how he could be in love with these two beautiful and successful people at the same time. Either one was a knockout. Taken together, their looks, brains and personalities were almost too much for one man to handle. Did Danielle have any inkling of Robert's feelings for Bailey and Bailey's feelings for Robert?

"Robert, when do you think you will see Bailey again?" Danielle blurted out as if she was reading his mind.

"I don't know. I guess I might if I go to the American Heart Association's meeting in the fall or some big meeting in the coming year," he said matter of factly.

Some big meeting in the coming year, Danielle reflected. Bet they will meet at the A.H.A. meeting in the fall. That is when it will happen. Danielle debated in her own mind whether to open that up for further discussion or let it lie. She decided to let it go for the time being. But Danielle wondered why such a beautiful and talented woman as Bailey wasn't seriously attached to someone. She decided to pursue that for conversation.

"Robert, why do you think Bailey isn't seriously attached to some man at the present time?"

"I don't know. Could be for a variety of reasons. There are other cardiologists, women cardiologists, and for that matter, other specialists who love their profession and haven't found someone who meets their high expectations. Or perhaps there is some other family or innate reason that a man isn't higher on their personal priorities at the present time. Perhaps there was some significant man recently in their lives and for a variety of reasons it didn't work out. As you know, Danielle, every person has a

155

unique story to tell."

Not to let a good story about a good woman die yet, Danielle continued, "Bailey strikes me as one of the most sophisticated women I have ever encountered, and as you know, I have spent a lot of time around a number of very talented women. She is A+."

"I agree," Robert responded. "She brings a lot to the table."

"What kind of guy would she fall in love with?"

"He would have to be bright, quick witted, confident, accomplished. He would have to be a unique nurturer. He couldn't be intimidated easily. He would need to have deep character dimensions and be extremely compassionate and understanding. Engaging. He would have to help and share with her on deep levels at multiple levels. Like an Olympic star who is a zero handicap in golf yet accomplished pianist or musician while being well known in his field as CEO, artist or a successful standout in some professional sphere. Maybe a well known minister, preacher, actor or businessman. In great health. Excellent manners. Sort of Godlike," Robert reflected.

"Like you, Robert," Danielle smartly retorted.

"I said zero golf handicap, an Olympic star, CEO," Robert offered, suggesting disqualifications for himself. "As one of the beautiful people yourself, Danielle, what do you think she would want?"

"I think you pretty well described the person, Robert. He would be a distinctive gentleman, understanding and offering unconditional love. I feel she conveys unconditional love. She seemed very conscious of every person she met. It was like she would envelope them, as if they were the only person on earth. I noticed it at the restaurant. It wasn't only with each of us. I noticed her openness with the doormen, the maitre'd, the waiters and waitresses. It was like everyone was someone. And the more she got to know you, the more she opened up. Didn't you feel that, Robert?"

"Yes, I think you are quite right. She was definitely in the flow with each person. And she could relate to multiple people on the same warm and open manner. It was like she was engaging you to be more open to receive the full potential of the moment and the relationship."

"She exemplified Martin Buber's 'I and thou.' I was significant because of her. The value of I is only fully grasped in the presence and interaction of the other. But of course I had the same impression of all five of us at dinner. Didn't you, Robert?"

"Yes I truly did. But we were in Colorado, lest we forget."

"Yes, that is true. It seems much warmer among the people here in Colorado than back home in Washington."

"It has to do with the pace of our lives in Washington, D.C. There is a different rhythm here. The pace is more open and relaxed, closer to nature. With the sun, the mountains, the lush grass, the cool refreshing air. It is all so invigorating, so stimulating. How can anyone not be taken in by the rarefied air?"

"I agree, it is why we need to spend more time in Colorado," Danielle said. "But you know, Kerry and Don were from California."

"I have always loved California, from San Diego, La Jolla, to Monterey, Big Sur with great spots in between."

"Like Palm Springs, Santa Barbara, Yosemite, Lake Tahoe, to cite a few."

"Our attitudes, backgrounds and experiences influence our lives. You and I look forward to delighting others and sharing in delight. That is an attitude. We have learned to respect people and enjoy the moment with them. Here we made time for it. We flowed in the delight and the joy."

"With an open respect for each other," she said.

"There is a certain environment that makes us more attentive thus enabling us to bring more of ourselves to each moment and each person. We have learned the value of connectedness. Our environment and experiences heighten our consciousness and allow us to create more rewarding moments."

"I think we were open to the possibilities of the moment, and thus better able to understand, trust and grasp the richness of each person and each experience. Oh Robert, I feel tingly. I've become more conscious of the air we breathe, the words we speak, the views and people we see."

"The packing we need to zip up," Robert added, smiling.

"I have made some warm bread and fixed us some fruit and juice."

"We should probably nourish our bodies just as we have our minds," he said. As he drank his juice, he thought of Bailey. No juice could match that first glass of orange juice with Bailey in her white robe.

As Danielle ate her fruit and fresh bread, it seemed as fresh and enjoyable as any bread and fruit ever tasted. Perhaps it was the conversation that made her more sensitive to everything she was doing.

"Danielle, this is a great breakfast. A fitting conclusion to our excellent stay. May it nourish us for the coming year."

"Well at least until we have lunch in a few hours," she added. "Robert what was the most rewarding moment of this vacation?"

He wanted to say meeting Bailey. "Having your fresh baked bread just now."

"You sound like President Jackson, well known for citing

her most recent encounter as the most significant."

"I am not that good a politician."

"But you did say my freshly baked bread."

"I guess the most significant thing for me is the possibility of a Colorado life, at least spending more time in the mountain or having similar mountain experiences."

"That's funny, because I was going to offer that as one of my take-aways. The other is our friendships with Bailey, Kerry and Don. Granted Bailey and you may have more in common. But I liked their western California/Colorado attitude. They were more plugged in to the moment, and conscious of it."

"Spontaneous, as our heart is spontaneous."

"Yes, Robert, spontaneous as our hearts. Although I think we in Washington do things from the heart spontaneously, I don't think we are always conscious of it. Life in Washington, D.C. can be as fast paced as New York, Chicago, Hong Kong or any other bustling metropolis and economy. We need more time to breathe, to treat each other as human beings on a regenerated and regenerative earth."

"Life sustaining, with a lot of fresh air."

"Yes, life sustaining. Life creating, with a lot more fresh air."

"We will bring this renewed attitude to Washington, D.C., Northern Virginia, the Shenandoah Valley, rural Maryland and beyond the beltway."

"Yes outside the beltway and beyond the Hill."

"Definitely, beyond the Hill."

"Robert, we truly are blessed. Just think of all the memories and experiences that we have shared in the last few minutes."

"Maybe we need some quiet time, just to reflect, and

capture the joy of the moment."

"Yes, to enjoy." They smiled and felt the enjoyment.

"I will load the car up while you clean up. Is that okay?" Robert asked.

"And if I say no?"

"Then, I will have to ask you to go to bed."

"Okay, that is a great idea."

* * * * *

A little while later they were in the car and headed east under a glorious morning sun.

"This is truly amazing. I will never cease to be awed by these mountains and Vail Valley."

"Yes, there are worse places on earth," Robert added.

"As we roll along Interstate 70 here for the next two hours, what changes do you see in our lives as we rebalance them?"

"Good question. Regarding our life together, I guess finding time together, and being the best we can be," he responded.

"Do you want a baby now?"

"More appropriately, Danielle, do you want a baby?"

She hesitated. "I think so, but I am not sure."

"Interesting response. Why do you think so and why aren't you sure?"

"The reason I think so is because I am not getting any younger and I always thought we would have children some day, and this seems almost as good as any time. I am not sure because I have tried to project one month, five months, nine months , even years out to imagine how it would be for me, for the child, for you, for us, and I have been so preoccupied with my work and our

160

relationship," quietly she contemplated her relationship with Senator Hart, "that I really hadn't thought about it as fully as I think I ought."

"Wasn't it the philosopher Descartes or Kant who dealt extensively with the oughts in our life?" Robert asked. "Well think out loud about how you think it would be one month out, five months out, nine months out, and one, five and nine years out."

"God, that is crazy isn't it. Can you see us with an eight year old? Girl or boy do you think, Robert?"

"Well what do you want?"

"As long as it is healthy, it can be either a girl or boy. And that's another thing I worry about. Can you imagine if the baby wasn't normal? I mean we would expect it to be, but imagine if it wasn't."

"We would still love the baby, Danielle."

"I know we would love her or him. But I wouldn't want to disappoint you or our family."

"I wouldn't worry about it, Danielle. The odds are that you will have a beautiful bright baby, spoiled beyond all get out. But still a great baby."

"Do you really think so? Of course you would. You are the most optimistic person on earth."

"Aren't I married to you, Danielle?"

"Yes, what does that mean?"

"You are the most, or second most, positive person on earth."

"Well, which is it?"

"You tell me."

"We'll be co-most positive."

"Sounds cool to me. So about the baby."

"About the baby, I think it is possible in the next year or two."

"Well, you will have to become more specific for me, Danielle."

"There you are, the precise cardiologist is coming out. Maybe we should make love on your birthday, create the baby then so the most positive person on earth can be an eternal flame."

"Danielle."

"Yes, Robert."

"Have you thought about the next many months and years?"

"One thought that occurs to me is how you would feel."

"The data indicates that a mother's dominant thoughts turn first to the children and then the spouse. That is only natural."

"So how would you feel about it, Robert?"

"If that is truly what you want, fine."

"But that doesn't express it for you, Robert."

"It does express it for me."

"I am sensing that it is of secondary importance to you, Robert."

"More importantly, Danielle, you need to project your own reality. I am fine with whatever reality you create, personally, family wise, or professionally."

"That doesn't strike me as projecting your preference, Robert, and I firmly believe you have a preference."

"My preference is your preference. You are the one I love and will love."

"But will you love me more with a baby or without?"

"Will you love me more with a baby or without?"

"That's not fair, Robert."

"Who said anything about fair. But now that you brought

it up, we both believe in being fair and just. That is why you opened this discussion up. Is it a win-win? Aren't we concerned about the endings, the ending of the pregnancy in nine months, the situation in nine, nineteen or for that matter ninety years?"

"I never really thought of it in those precise perspectives. But yes I want to project nine months to the birth of the baby, nine years to the growth of the baby, nineteen as a teenager, and ninety years to an elder. Wouldn't a baby enrich all of our lives?"

"If you think yes and I think yes then let us enrich ourselves. I just want you to create those projected realities, to realize as much potential as you can, for yourself, myself, the baby and all who would share in the birth and life of our baby. The other concern I have is, are you ready to modify your professional relationship with the Women's Health Caucus? Can they grow in the coming year without you for six weeks to three or more months? How will you feel during such a hiatus? Will you have any regrets? Will you feel any different, any better? How will all others feel?"

"Robert, I don't know. None of us are indispensable. You know that. We may seem indispensable in some relationships, but we can all survive. We may evolve as a result of it. What about spontaneity, Robert? Earlier we were talking about spontaneity, it has great value too."

"Let's stop the car, climb in the backseat and make love, Danielle."

"Are you serious, Robert?"

"Serious. Delirious. That would be spontaneous."

"I am almost tempted to take you up on it. I left my underwear off purposely," Danielle said.

"You didn't."

"I did."

"Show me."

Calling his bluff, she unzipped her shorts and displayed her womb...no underwear.

"You are more woman than I ever realized. No myth with you or is there?"

Silence reigned for a while. Robert smiled. He wondered what on earth provoked her to wear no underwear. Did she do this often? Had anyone else provoked her not to wear underwear? Don or some other guy here in Colorado? Was it a Senator, Representative or one of their aides?

Danielle simultaneously wondered whether she had stimulated Robert. Was he provoked positively or negatively? Was this unconditional love? Or was this surrender? Surely it was spontaneous or did Danielle, in her refined calculating way, set Robert up to make love and have a baby? Was she calling his bluff? Or calling her bluff? She obviously hadn't considered the series of questions Robert had thrown at her. Was she going to consider them all? Was it too calculating to do so? Or was it blind emotion and raw passion to provoke Robert to make love to her now? Would they miss their plane? It wasn't like these two intellectually analytical professionals to act spontaneously.

"So Danielle, what are you thinking?"

"Should I think, Robert? Or just be?"

"Just be. You and me. I am also not wearing underwear."

She laughed. "You have no underwear on? Do you regularly wear no underwear?"

"I wore torn underwear, so you could easily rip them off."

"Sure."

"No kidding."

"To make love and make a baby."

"What will be will be. Que sera sera."

"Let me see."

"Really."

"I need to see the distinguished cardiologist with torn underwear."

"To be ripped further by the successful professional woman desirous of making her baby on the road through the mountains."

"Let me see."

Robert disclosed a tear on the top of the boxer shorts right under the waistband.

"Great. You win, I win. It is the great American experience." She laughed.

"Well, Danielle, give me some more answers to my projected questions, especially those about you and the caucus."

"I am contemplating all of it." She looked longing at him with her head slightly cocked to its side, and then stared out of her side window. "I think it would be revealing to many, including myself, if we had a baby soon. The caucus would be shocked, but others would be pleasantly surprised. They all believe in love. Most everyone believes strongly in having and nurturing babies and raising them appropriately with unconditional love. My life would be changed. I don't know exactly how, but I have never known exactly how, even with my past professional and unpredictable political life."

"It would be a changed you. A new you. But maybe it's what people expect of you, even if they haven't expressed it."

"What makes you say that, Robert?"

"Well, you are the prototype superwoman. You have done it all. You are beautiful, independent, smart, politically adept, professionally successful. You have had several professions and could do several more. Personally you have nurtured thousands of people. So why not nurture your own children?"

"My own children?"

"Yes."

"You see us with more than one child?"

"I can't see having only one child. It would be an injustice. Unless you could have no more. Then I would understand."

"I guess if we had one, we could easily have several. I think when you and I to do something, we want to do it to the fullest. Having more than one child would be doing family to the fullest. We are two good people who have much to give to others. We have already done much for others. So it may be time to give ourselves to our children who can do more for the world for a longer period of time and to a greater extent than you and I can or will."

"Are you questioning our capabilities as human beings, Danielle?"

"Yes I guess I am. We may have five or six decades to live. Our children will have great opportunity to give to others for, perhaps, over one hundred to one hundred and thirty years. And just think if we have three or four."

"Or more children, as we have discussed before."

"Well what do you think, Robert, should we have three, four or more?"

"How about two, a boy and a girl, the All American family?"

"Is that all you want? What if we had two boys or two girls, would you then want more?"

"Two is fine. One for you and one for me. That way we can focus our energy and talents in the most responsible way."

"You're serious, Robert? Just two? Earlier you said six, four natural and two adopted."

"Actually, Danielle. I am quite open to the number of children, whether you bring them into the world or we adopt. I think we have much to give to children. I am sure we would be challenged in the process as well," he said.

"No doubt we would be challenged and I am open to adoption as well, but like most women, I think I would like to bear at least one or two, maybe three children, into the world."

"You mean, see how it goes with the first one or two children and then decide whether to have more?"

"Yes. I think that might make sense, don't you?" she asked.

"Sure. I guess the critical thing is when to begin."

"Yes, when and how."

"And how?"

"Like now, with no or torn underwear."

"Well mine feels comfortable, how about you?"

"I feel very comfortable. In fact I am glad we have had this extensive discussion. Especially in these beautiful Colorado mountains."

"Yes the environment facilitates open discussion in a relaxed atmosphere. I am glad we discussed this subject here."

"Well we have known each other for over a dozen years, so it might have been better to have discussed it earlier."

"I guess we have had more than ample time. People should think more deeply about having children, than they do. And they need to be better prepared."

"Yes, whatever that is."

"What I mean, Danielle is that our child would intervene in our lives much more than we realize. Don't you agree?"

"Yes, but you could spend a lifetime considering how to do it best and then never have them."

"You're right and people do."

"Well, Robert, are you ready to take me in your arms and have a baby now?"

"Give me a few minutes to consider," he said, as they drove uphill towards Eisenhower Tunnel.

"Knowing you, you would probably like to do it in the tunnel."

"Now, Danielle, what makes you say that?"

"Well, it's not in sunlight."

"I love sunlight."

"It's different."

"You are right there. I guess I would be concerned about the lack of space and the flow of traffic inside the tunnel."

"Always concerned about the details, Robert, aren't you?"

"Well, if there was an alcove or something. Or maybe, we could leave the car parked outside the tunnel and walk in, get to one of those guard's perches along the wall and do it in there as the cars whisked by."

"Great, I love it. When we drive through the tunnel, will you please describe, blow by blow, how we would do it in the cramped space of one of those guard's perches?"

"Definitely."

"Well, Robert, if not in the tunnel, where?"

"We could do it in Silver Plumb or Georgetown. That might be apropos for a number of reasons. Silver Plumb because of its historical railroad. We might create a great engineer there. We could call him or her our silver plumb. In Georgetown, because it is a great university, and a great community back east. We would surely create a great individual there."

"Like a cardiologist."

"We wouldn't want to put that kind of burden on the

168

individual."

"Well which is it, Robert, Silver Plumb or Georgetown?"

"What about Winter Park? It is so beautiful."

"Winter Park. I like the connotations. We heated up the winter season when we decided to park. It would be great encouragement to other lovers and romantics."

"Actually, any of those suggestions are good ones. What place do you like?"

"What about if we get off first in Silver Plumb, check it out. See if we can find some great place to make love. And if not, then proceed to Georgetown, follow the same process, look for a place we like, if not found, we move on to the trail to Winter Park."

"I like it."

"You like me. I like you. And I want to make love to you as soon as possible," Danielle felt herself heat up. She sensed the moistness of the moment.

Robert similarly became more solid in his position, to make love and have a baby, here and now in the mountains.

The day never seemed more glorious. The sun was beaming across a beautiful blue sky spotted with cotton ball clouds. The river below rushed downstream. The wildflowers along the highway were like bouquets from heaven. The tall fir trees never stood straighter. Tens of thousands of them along the highway, ever so erect in their vigil of the Holy Family as they proceeded down the highway looking for the loving inn that would take them in. The air, with eighty degree temperature and a slight breeze, was perfect for this impending personal encounter of the highest dimension.

They reached Silver Plumb. Danielle touched Robert's thigh.

"Robert, are you as anxious and exhilarated as I am?"

"Yes, I am," he responded, feeling the warmth of her hand on his leg.

"What are you feeling, Robert?" she asked as they pulled off Interstate 70 and into the little mountain town.

"I want to find a nice comfortable place to tear your clothes off and feel you as intimately as we have ever felt each other," he said.

As they turned off they noticed residential homes and a few stores. On their left they saw the Peak Inn. It looked perfect.

They parked the car and entered this quaint little inn that looked like an old rambling single home. A friendly man about seventy years of age sitting in the beautiful, screen-enclosed front porch beckoned them in.

"Come right in, come right in," he said.

"Hi, how are you?" Robert and Danielle said.

"Wonderful. Can I help you with a room?"

"Yes, can we see the best in the house. And what's the rate?" Robert pursued.

"Sure, sure. I'll show you our honeymoon suite. It's $95 a night."

Robert and Danielle nodded approvingly, site yet unseen. They probably would have paid anything at this point.

Up the stairs they proceeded to a room at the end of the hallway. The door opened to a good sized master suite with big open windows looking out on the surrounding mountains. Robert was first to try out the bed.

"Seems good," he remarked as he bounced up and down.

"Yes, this is great," Danielle offered as she sat on the other side of the bed.

"Then this will do," the innkeeper confirmed.

"Perfect. You have a deal," Robert said.

"Well, come downstairs and we'll do the paperwork."

They returned downstairs and completed the paperwork. Robert paid cash for the room.

"Can I help you with your bags?" the innkeeper inquired.

"No that's not necessary sir. We just want the room to make love, create a baby and expand our love horizon."

"Well, to each his own," the innkeeper chimed in. "It is a great bed and a great room to make love in. You probably noticed the white bear rug on the floor."

"Yes, we did. That's a great touch," Robert said.

Robert and Danielle walked down the hall and up the stairs. Danielle was first up the stairs, her athletic legs and buttocks assertively climbing towards paradise. Robert was right behind her, viewing his wife's physique and dreaming of her fully naked body in his arms.

As soon as Danielle was in the room, she pulled her blouse over her head revealing her beautiful breasts. She was braless. She spun around and faced Robert.

"Take me, I want to make love with you," she exclaimed.

Robert took off his Colorado Rockies T-shirt, revealing an athletic, bronzed chest. They passionately embraced and exchanged a long, wet and passionate kiss, as if they were two lovers who had not seen each other for a long time. Robert squeezed her tight with his right hand firmly in the square of her back, and his left hand pressed against her head, slowly working that hand through her soft and flowing hair.

Danielle pressed against Robert with all her might, her right hand feeling the strength of his lower back, her left hand at his neck, squeezing her fingers into the lower back of his neck, combining the sweat of her hand with his sweat, binding the two of them in an intimate embrace.

After long passionate kisses and embraces, each expressing themselves in loving, gentle and raw sexual ways their love for one another was fully exposed.

Robert let his left hand drop to Danielle's buttocks. His other hand fell to the lower part of her back and side.

Danielle moved her right hand down his still belted blue jeans, savagely working her hand beneath the belt in the back, feeling the shorts she would soon rip off. With her left hand, she unbuckled his belt and slowly unzipped his pants.

Feeling his wife's raw passion and strength, Robert opened her front belt and unzipped her tight shorts, exposing her inviting body.

They tumbled to the floor, she with her shorts at her knees, he with jeans at his ankles. They both laughed, squeezed each other tightly and helped each other undress.

Danielle, completely naked, saw Robert standing before her with his underwear. She spotted the tear under his waistband, grabbed it ferociously and tore it open to reveal all of Robert.

They both laughed again and then seriously and passionately embraced on the soft white bearskin rug. Robert, with only remnants of his shorts still on him, pressed his body hard on top of her. Danielle, ever quick and agile, rolled him over, to take the dominant position. Freer on top, she picked up her head and upper torso, better to view him with her legs straddling outside of his legs. She kissed him on his legs, forehead, shoulders, chest, stomach, everywhere. She was having fun loving the man she married and with whom she wanted her baby.

Within a short period of time, he was back on top. Now it was his turn to kiss her, starting with the lips and forehead, down to her shoulders, her breasts, and bronzed belly. They were ready.

She wanted him. She wanted him badly. And he was ready to bring her a new life as mother and wife. They met with a joyous thunder and climax. And then there was three. Or at least that's what they felt.

It was joyous and fulfilling for both of them. They hugged and squeezed each other. They kissed and teased and fussed over each other. They were quite at peace with one another on the white bearskin rug. It felt like they could stay there forever. They kept eyeing and touching one another, knowing that a new life was beginning for them. The window to the room was open. They could hear the light breeze blowing through the leaves of the aspens. They tussled each other's hair. There was a gentle softness to the moment. It was as if the world decided to stop for them.

Danielle, still playing with Robert's hair, was the first to break the silence. "Robert, how long do you think we will stay here? I know we left with plenty of time to catch our plane. But is that still possible if we stay here much longer?"

"Yes, we can still stay here a little while. We left about four hours before take-off. We have to return the car, so we probably don't want to stay more than another 30 minutes. I presume you want to catch that flight, because I don't know what the availability of later flights is. Usually in August there is pretty heavy traffic back east from Denver late on a Sunday. Everyone is trying to extend the daylight time in Colorado as much as possible before they take-off from here, wishing to get back by late Sunday evening. I can call the airline to see what the possibility is for catching a later flight. It will only cost about seventy-five dollars extra per ticket."

"Yes, Robert, why don't you call. It would be nice if we had an extra few hours to be in each other's arms."

"Okay." He reached for his airline pocket guide, found the phone number for United Airlines and called it. "Hello, we have a reservation on the next flight from Denver to Washington, D.C. and are wondering what the possibility is for us to catch a later flight this afternoon or earlier this evening."

He listened. "Yes, I will wait while you check." He stroked Danielle's cheek with his fingertips. "Great, so both flights are open, the three thirty and the six thirty." Turning to Danielle, "do you want to catch the six thirty, we don't arrive until eleven forty five? Or do you want the three thirty which gets us in at eight forty five tonight?"

"Let's take the three thirty. That gives us over three more hours and we will get in at a more reasonable time."

"Fine, put us both on your three thirty." He listened again. "Great, thanks again."

Robert turned towards Danielle who was anxious to get passionate again, knowing she had three more hours of this paradise. She began kissing and caressing him. Before long they were repeating their earlier sizzling encounter. But this time they were on the bed. They ravished each other, challenging their energies and endurance. They embraced in a body-to-body hug. It was unbelievable how they could recreate the passion that they had just experienced. Like endurance athletes they extended the limits of their physical, emotional and psychological capabilities. Within minutes they were again reaching the peaks of human ability. And Danielle was demanding the utmost of her lover. As if timed, they peaked at the same time, and finally climaxed as if to seal the destiny of their initial baby creation, in case there were any doubts.

Panting fully and rhythmically, Robert and Danielle sounded like synchronized swimmers. They felt the intense heat and sweat from their lovemaking, and ran their hands along each other's impassioned bodies. How could life be so good, Danielle thought. In parallel fashion, Robert thought this was the only way to spend a Sunday afternoon.

After a few minutes of resting, lying side by side, and staring at the spouse they had chosen more than twelve years ago, each was as close to human ecstasy as possible. Could they go at it a third time? It had been over eleven years since they were able to do it three times within the same day. But it wasn't necessary because they had already exceeded their expectations.

"Robert," she said, "I am sure we created a new life, aren't you?"

"Without a doubt."

"Do you think it is a boy or a girl?"

"From the way you contributed to the enterprise, Danielle, I think it is a girl. But, I felt like I fired real bullets, so it could be a boy."

"Maybe it's twins, a boy and a girl."

"Now that would be something. My first cousins are triplets, and I know there are twins on your side of the family."

"I am sure if we are ready for one child, we can just as easily be ready for two."

"Our lives are going to be changed by a child. Do you think having two children is going to make much difference?"

"I don't think it would make much difference. I will take six to twelve weeks off with the birth, and then probably return to work full time. That is if everything works out alright."

"Being flexible."

"Being flexible is good, Robert. The ability to deal with ambiguity is one of the great demands of our time. I am ready for whatever the future brings us. Love endures all, right Robert?"

"Love endures all, Danielle."

Chapter Nine
Reevaluate Love

The rest of the ride down the mountain was relatively uneventful. Uneventful, if you call a car ride from ecstasy the normal course.

The sun was still beaming. Temperature might have been eighty-one degrees. Their body heat had to be in excess of one hundred degrees. Each sat in the car as before, except Danielle wore no underwear and Robert was in new, untorn ones. Robert was at peace. Danielle was churning like a hot barbecue charcoal.

"Robert, thank you so much for this day. It really is a high point in my life. I didn't know I could feel this way. It is unbelievable."

"You are more than welcome, Danielle. I have always felt blessed with my life, but this is among the greatest days of my life."

"For me perhaps number one or two," Danielle said.

"You mean we will have to create a priority rating?"

"Well what do you think?"

"I think a great, great day."

"No reason to rate in a competitive way, not when you have had a transcending collaboration as we enjoyed."

"We did enjoy it, didn't we?"

"Are you ready to stop again?"

"No, I am in ecstasy already, Danielle."

"I know what you mean, Robert. But I still want more of you. It was too good to be true."

"It was true, as true as truth gets."

"That's for sure, at least for us humans."

"Yes, for immortal beings it is an everyday occurrence.

176

But for us mere mortals, it was a slice of heaven, and it still is."

"Robert, did you ever think love could offer so much? That it could be so rich?"

"I think we have experienced an extraordinary amount of love, beginning with our childhood, and now in adulthood."

"When I think of my childhood, Robert, I think of how patient and kind my parents were, especially with me between the ages of twelve and twenty-two. Even when I arrogantly believed I knew better than either one of them. I never once saw my parents jealous of one another or of others. They were never boastful, but allowed me and my sisters to express our boastful selves, especially when we were teenagers. I often insisted on having my own way. They could have easily restricted our behavior. Instead, they taught us right from wrong. Sometimes we resented the fact that they knew better, although we seldom admitted it."

"That's how it was for me and my siblings. I also remember the joys and triumphs we enjoyed."

"Oh, I do too, Robert. I remember several times, when I did something right or achieved something significant, a milestone, our family celebrated. My sisters and I were blessed with great parents and many successes."

"Our parents took a lot from me and my brothers and sister. We often challenged the status quo and tested our limits. But our parents believed in us. No matter what we did, they believed that we would recognize what was good or right in any situation. For us, and for others. And if we made a mistake, they believed that given time we would learn and see the light. They believed in us, so we naturally believed in ourselves. To have someone believe in you is one of the best things in life. Belief transcends any one of us. It is an inspiration in life. Belief is the inspiration. It is the spirit that transcends any wrongdoing, any weakness that might exist in our life."

"Robert, my mother and father felt and thought similarly about hope. Hope would transcend all. Hope, like belief, would see you through. As many ministers are apt to say. Keep hope alive. Keep hope alive. Hope is alive. Hope will see you through, no matter how dark it might seem. Love nurtures hope. It makes you believe in yourself. Love encompasses hope and belief. We have been so blessed to love, be loved, hope in another, have another hope in us, believe in one another, and have another believe in us."

"Have many others believe and hope in us and we in them," Robert added.

At that moment Robert and Danielle looked at each other. The attraction between the two was unmistakable. Their love was unconditional. The beneficiary would be their new child.

"Robert, have you ever tried to comprehend the powers and influences in our lives?"

"Often. The power and influence of my mom and dad, my brothers, my aunts and uncles was genuine and exceptional. And along the way, many professors and mentors also shared their power and influence. Theirs was true love. That is the only way to describe it."

"There are so many people who gave so much of themselves in our lives. And the giving seemed unconditional. It was always there in one form or shape. Often times we didn't recognize it, didn't appreciate it because we weren't open to it. Openness is so key to growing, to loving, to being loved," said Danielle. She then began to more deeply reflect on this thought. "It has a qualitative nature that is hard to define or to specify. You and I have felt it, experienced it. It is a quality of life that permeates the air, infiltrates the spirit, actually spoils one who experiences it."

"There is no doubt we have been loved by people with extremely big hearts and enormous human spirits. My father told me of Max Scheler, a German philosopher, who wrote of ordo amoris, the order of the heart. The heart you know has a high order to it. Those with disordered hearts experience resentment, 'resentiment' as Scheler stated it, and they bring resentment to other people and life experiences," Robert offered.

"My parents always saw life and love as intertwined. Living and loving, that's what mattered. Love was independent and yet we all shared in it. It created an interdependence among us, yet ignited inner growth. Love was the glue of life," Danielle remarked.

"Yes, the glue of life, a sticky material felt in love making that ignited everything in its path. Love turned everything warm. Love heated the coldest days, the coldest hearts," Robert contributed.

"I have seen hardened people soften in the presence of love. I remember my mother expressing her love for each of us in every phone call and in every letter she wrote. 'Hug everyone,' she would say. 'Tell them I love them. Think about you dear,' she would say. 'Think about everyone. Love everyone. Express your love in everything you say and do. Love is the ultimate expression. Love is the ultimate gift.' And to tease her I would say 'is it better than a walk down Worth Avenue in Palm Beach or Fifth Avenue in Naples?' She would respond, 'Unless you walk on the wild side.'"

"'Walk on the wild side, Mommy?'" I would ask.

"'On the wild side of love where all of God's people, animals and creatures have the opportunity to love and be loved,' she would say. And we would quietly reflect on the wild side of

179

love, especially when we walked on Worth Avenue in Palm Beach or on Fifth Avenue in Naples."

"How often would you walk on Worth Avenue or on Fifth Avenue?" Robert inquired.

"Every couple of years. Daddy loved the sun. He loved to go down south especially Florida, sometimes Arizona or California. Daddy encouraged us to be in the sun whenever we could. He said it was a life force. An energy source that ignited love. And Mom would second that. Of course, he loved us even when the sun wasn't shining. But when the sun was shining, God's love glistened upon the earth and ignited love, just like spring jump-starts all human souls and flowers."

"It truly is powerful. Think of the rising and setting suns we have seen this vacation. The beauty of the sun in the morning as it came over the mountains in the east. And then those glorious evenings with the sun creating magnificent pictures in the West, each a little different from the day before. The beauty and power of the sun, like love, is undeniable," Robert sighed.

"Robert, your love for me is undeniable, and I thank you for that. It sustains and enhances me."

"You're welcome, Danielle. You do the same for me. It is unbelievable to experience such deep, personal love. Thank you, my dear. I don't know of another woman who could love me the way you do." No sooner had Robert said this than a picture of Bailey appeared in his consciousness. He was struck by it, and at the same time he was able to evoke a warm simple feeling towards Danielle.

Simultaneously, as Robert spoke she thought of Senator Hart while at the same time feeling love for Robert. How could someone feel such piercing love from two men? Danielle was surprised by the joy and delight both men gave her. She felt

180

overwhelmed by emotion, and sizzled with warmth and love. This was crazy. How could one woman be so turned on, so loved, and so in love with two wonderful and powerful men? She enjoyed it, took delight in it. At the same time she was worried. Would she be able to continue loving two men unconditionally even after having the child of one of them?

Robert engaged in sizzling thoughts of his own. Two fabulous women preoccupied his brain and his heart. Danielle and Bailey. How could this be? It was. And Robert had created it by being open to both women. He truly loved his wife. Unconditionally. Yet, Bailey, a woman who shared much in common with him, personally and professionally, was encompassing his emotions and his thoughts. She was physically distanced from him now, but could easily be brought alive in the studio of his heart and mind. She, like Danielle, was truly an exceptional woman. A woman to be loved. How could he be more attentive, more focused on loving these two women? That was crazy. Ironically, he had experienced one of the highlights of his life on this day with his wife. He couldn't have been more involved or more committed than he had just been with Danielle. His consciousness was at an ultimate high. The experience was the most rewarding, the most creative. Everything was at ultimate flow. Understanding was maximized, the possibilities and choices unleashed. Robert's thoughts raced to fulfilling his two loves, each to the maximum. That was impossible, and he knew it. But, didn't he also believe that anything was possible?

Robert was now faced with clarifying his goals in each relationship. The challenge would be maintaining clear and constant communication with both Danielle and Bailey. Feelings were obviously out of control. At least they were all positive ones. Robert had the greatest challenge a man could face. Deep within him was the motivation to do the best he could given the situation. The challenge now was how to be open to each moment with Danielle and Bailey... how to fully interact with both of them. The risk was limiting the full potential of each relationship in terms of creative demand. How could Robert maintain and be most sensitive to the needs of Danielle, Bailey, himself, patients, colleagues, staff and friends? How could the human dimension of each personality, each relationship be maximized to its potential? Robert had a tremendous personal and professional ability to enhance and expand every human relationship he had encountered. He and Danielle had helped each other grow personally and professionally. Their circle of friends had benefited by Robert's and Danielle's interactions. Danielle and Robert with all their skill and ability had focused on developing as human beings and helping others develop as well.

Significant questions were now before them.

"Danielle, how can we love each other more, from this day forward?" Robert asked, breaking the steamy silence.

"What, a question!" exclaimed Danielle. "What exactly do you mean, Robert?"

"Well, Danielle, how can I help you? How can I serve you better?"

"Such questions! How can you help me, Robert, goodness. Well, we can lay in bed longer, we can make more love. We can stroke each other longer...and softer. We can look into each other's eyes longer. We can feel each other deeper and in different ways. We can see more sunrises and sunsets together."

"Interesting. Each thing you identified seemed to be connected to a longer time period."

"Isn't that what values are about? What endures? What endures longer and deeper?"

"Yes, yes it does. But we have such minimal free time. In fact, our lives are but a speck of sand in the time continuum."

"Very rich specks of sand."

"Yes they are."

"Robert, how can I help you? How can I serve and nurture you?"

"Let me think about it. I know I initiated this ridiculously demanding series of questions." After a few moments Robert continued. "I guess just loving and caring for me, thinking of me, talking with me, being considerate of me, respecting me and helping me grow."

"And do you want to hold me and squeeze me and keep telling me you love me?"

"I love to hold you and squeeze you and tell you I love you as we have been doing. That's easy to do."

"Well do it boy, do it. Because I love it."

"And we don't do it often enough. It is truly a great joy to be in your arms, a warm embrace enhanced by the sun."

"Enhanced by the sun."

"Robert, am I the most important person in your life?"

Without pause, Robert responded, "Yes, you are." The picture of Bailey at Arrowhead appeared prominently in Robert's head. "Am I the most important person in your life, Danielle?"

"Definitely," Danielle immediately responded, yet she too was thinking of Senator Hart.

"Do you think we will continue to be the most important person in each other's lives?"

Danielle paused, then responded matter of factly, "Yes I do. Don't you?"

"Yes, probably." he said.

"Probably?"

"More than likely," he said.

"More than likely?" she dug even deeper. Now she was curious, as any woman would be, especially the wife.

He laughed.

"More than likely," she murmured under her breath.

But she didn't think it was funny.

"It is a rather compassioned and impassioned response," Robert understood that although his response was honest, it was not the most loving.

"The interesting thing about what you said, Robert, is the fact that you shared it with me. That is what love is all about," Danielle responded in a rather enlightened way.

"You are absolutely right Danielle, love means sharing truth. It is very difficult for people to share. The risk seems too great. But to give is to get, and people don't realize how much they have to give. Some people don't know what to give or how to give. The richness of life should be shared, explored, found. How can we enrich life even more?" Robert inquired.

"We enrich it by nurturing it. We nurture it by loving it. Attending to it. Listening. Responding. Inspiring others and being open to another's inspiration. Celebrating."

"Yes, by celebrating. That's it, Danielle. We should not only celebrate birthdays, anniversaries and graduations, but also create new ceremonies and rituals, fill life with surprises, celebrate life everyday."

"Celebration is such a wonderful word. It's so full of life, so merry. Life is a celebration everyday with the dawning of a new day and the setting of a new sun. We also celebrate life by loving everyone in every way everyday. That sounds like my mother."

"And my mother."

"And my father."

"And my father too."

"Sounds like a prayer. A prayer and a life full of love," Danielle shared.

"Yes, a life full of love that both of us have experienced with our families. We have been quite fortunate. We need to express our gratitude more often."

"Yes celebrate a life full of gratitude. May others be as fortunate as you and me, and love and share and celebrate with one another."

They became silent. Danielle looked out of the passenger window.

"Well I guess it is time to be a little more responsible in our lives," Robert reflected as he began to think about returning to his cardiology practice.

"It has been great sharing this time with you, Robert. We have been responsible to each other."

"You're right, Danielle. In our lives we must balance personal and professional responsibilities. And sometimes, those of us in America may tip the balance to the professional side, at the expense of our personal lives. I know that is true of a number of my colleagues."

"And it is true of my colleagues and friends in Washington and around the world."

"Yes, it is very true of Washington, D.C."

"Washington is often unbalanced, favoring professional preoccupations and denying the personal dimension. Yet, like in no other town in the world, its vast resources allow us to create possibilities for humans in the United States and the world," Danielle added.

"I guess that is one of the reasons why you and I and others like us live in Washington, D.C. We love the challenge of creating human possibilities in a town of human impossibilities."

"The personal dimension is greatly challenged in a town of such concentrated world power, a world of very bright and talented people challenged by their egos."

"It reminds me of that television program my folks used to watch called the Naked City, set in New York. The beginning of the show opened with the line, 'In this city, there are eight million stories. This is one of them,'" Robert relayed.

"That's appropriate for Washington. There are at least eight million stories. Most people in this town have hundreds of stories themselves, when one considers all the complex individual interactions among people in the government agencies, the White House, Congress, and all of the quasi-public agencies and groups. And then consider the myriad of private groups, like mine and thousands like it. Associations. Nonprofits. And the Universities. Not only yours and all those originally in Washington, D.C., but those from the University of Southern California who have graduate programs here," Danielle added.

"And all of the international groups."

"Yes, the international groups, the embassies, the visitors, domestic and international."

"It is a wonderful city," Robert exclaimed.

"You know, reflecting on responsibility, this country is in dire need of leadership. At times it seems there is a moral vacuum."

"Well, there is no incentive to be a leader in Washington, D.C. unless you consider yourself. I consider you to be a leader."

"Well, aren't you sweet, Robert. But I have my frailties and weaknesses, my imperfections too, Robert. I see you as a leader. A powerful man in medicine, pushing the limits of our knowledge base in the heart."

"Well, in some ways, we were given certain talents and abilities to contribute to the stewardship of others."

"You mean we try to be responsible."

"As we were saying earlier, we try to be responsible to each other, to other people and to our God-given talents and human potential," Robert shared.

"Responsibility is just a little discipline mixed with a little hard work."

"We are not conveying the need for leadership in this country, or creating incentives for leaders to emerge in every facet of our society. Although, leadership is its own reward, we need to instill the need for leadership in the minds of individuals."

"Why not create more leadership models, in primary and secondary school, as well as in college? We could foster graduate programs in leadership and stewardship as well," Danielle stated.

"Schools of self-mastery."

"Schools of self-mastery."

"There is a Center for Creative Leadership in North Carolina."

"I know. I inquired there once about a position and have had staff attend their courses."

"There needs to be more of those kinds of schools, especially those that offer programs in public service," Robert contributed.

"For too long public service has not been given the respect it deserves."

"Great leaders are responsible people, thoughtful of others, and dedicated to making things better for others."

"Those people clean up the messes that the less-considerate create by helping the needy with health care, education, employment or housing."

"Well that's you Danielle. You have been involved for a lifetime helping others in need."

"Yes, but I and others need to do more. Those in need of health insurance surpasses forty million people. That is a disgrace in this leading democracy. And the right wing doesn't help matters. Those forty million people, most of them women and children, deserve better. Most of them are poor, without jobs. Some just got laid off from the current merger mania. Or are going bankrupt, having credit problems. They need help. They need our help and the help of everyone in America. No one in America should go to bed hungry, homeless or without some love in their life. We need a national agenda of love. Share the wealth. Share the love. Share the talents and resources of those who have them. Especially now that more talented people are retiring earlier with great talents, skills and resources to share. Let's have a national agenda of love and sharing. We can address every problem in America if we set our minds and hearts to it. It should be a national agenda for responsible love, led by the President of the United States with the support of Congress and corporate America. Schools, colleges and universities should make it their number one priority."

"Danielle, you should run for higher office on a platform of responsible love."

"As soon as I feel I am a responsible lover, I will."

They both laughed. Deep down each knew of their imperfections. They were generally responsible and had the needed talents and resource to perfect themselves. But it wouldn't happen overnight or soon.

Truthfulness was the challenge for both Robert and Danielle. Perfect truthfulness seemed impossible to achieve.

Honesty was in such demand in the world. In America. In Washington, D.C.

"You know these courses and programs in leadership we were talking about earlier. They need to have majors in honesty and truthfulness. It is such a challenge to be totally honest and truthful in today's society. Why is that? How can we make it better?"

"Honesty and truthfulness are right at the core of love. I believe the greatest lovers of our time are those who were truthful and honest with themselves. Think of the great leaders you know, Danielle, aren't they the most honest and truthful?"

"I don't know. I imagine so. But the statistics I have seen about lying in America are astounding."

"I know. I have seen the same statistics and stories. In research today they are uncovering invalid and distorted data...more of it then ever before. Perhaps it is the pace and pressure of today's society that is testing our limits."

"Yes it may be, but that is no excuse. Sincerity and integrity are needed in life like never before. It is the basis for all human interactions." Danielle felt torn inside regarding her own sincerity and integrity. God knew how she tried to be truthful and honest, but it was that element of non-expression, what she kept inside, that was suspect. She did not know how to make it better. If she was truthful now, there would be dire consequences. She needed to keep learning. It was not always a win-win world. Danielle had learned that at an early age. She knew it was a win-learn world. She won most of the time. And she wanted others to win too. The reality was that sometimes you lost. You could always learn. Yes it was a win-learn world. Danielle was determined to focus on learning and helping others learn, including Robert. "The challenge for everyone is being truthful, honest and sincere," Danielle continued. "The challenge is it isn't always a black and white world. There are cloudy days, gray times. There are many differing views on almost every topic. And we are not talking about what is legal. That is a whole other thing. We are talking about something that transcends the law. No law can see a man or a woman's brain and heart and tell what is right and wrong. The legal system can and does serve a purpose, but for society to survive it must appeal to an honesty that transcends the law. And that is the challenge for every human being, for every community to be as truthful and as honest as possible."

"It is called being fair," Robert interpreted. "Being fair to one another. To consider the endings in every relationship. An ending that does not end. That is open regardless of the beginning, the middle or the end. Because if you are conscious of the ending, you are most conscious. The best ending is an open one. Open to one another regardless of what has transpired before."

"There is a social equity question we are talking about here," Danielle knew because she herself was focusing on being fair. To herself. To Robert. To Senator Hart. To everyone she knew. She thought often about how to enhance herself personally. Enhance her relationship with Robert. She loved the word enhance. It had an inspiration, an aspiration feel to it. En-hance. To bring to a higher level than before. She felt her life was enriched, enhanced. There was a new balance to it. A balance of personal and professional dimensions. There was an effort put forward to enhance the other, to be fair to all. There was a loyalty to this principle. It had structure. Trying for the win, knowing win-learn needed to be encouraged. Trying to enhance oneself and the other. Thinking of the ending of the relationship at the beginning and being open at the end to whatever relationship was encountered, knowing that openness would always enhance the future.

"Danielle," Robert inquired, "doesn't it all come down to our respect for life?"

"Yes, I think that is key," Danielle responded. "If we respect life, we sustain it. We must sustain it. There seems to be so little respect for life. If we respected life, we would be more honest and truthful. And vice versa, if we were more honest and truthful, we would express more respect for one another. I often think that the rich have little respect for the poor. And vice versa. But it seems to me that the rich have a heavier burden. I guess that is why it is written in the Bible that it will be more difficult for the rich to enter the kingdom of heaven. If the rich of Worth Avenue respected the poor of Palm Beach County, those poor neighborhoods would disappear with the help of the right leadership in public service."

"Danielle, you are such an optimist, such a dreamer, I love it."

"But it is true Robert. It could be true."

"I know. And we need to protect the environment and the people in it."

"True. If we protect the environment, we are showing respect for it. There is a certain decency to it."

"Decency, that is a good word, not often used. It is like sacred or respect. We need to return to what is truly decent and sacred."

"Today, America's religion is played out in our shopping malls. The shopping mall is the new church. That is a disgusting thought. Maybe if we just shut all the malls one weekend and asked everyone to think of the sacred, we would live in a better world."

"We don't give thanks enough. Danielle, thank you for

this vacation, this time together."
"Thank you for the sacred time we shared. It was lovely. I loved it, and I love you, Robert." At that moment she felt at home, loved, warm inside and out.
"Danielle, we have a wonderful relationship and I treasure it very much."
"I treasure you, Robert. I treasure you like Fort Knox with all of its gold bullion," she said never having been there. She didn't know why she said that, and remembered that the value of gold had fallen lately. "Robert, I love you more than gold," she said.
"I know you do, Danielle, because you have never been hung up on gold and related trappings."
"I guess you are right. We all need to focus more on the internal and be thankful for all that we have as individuals. We have so much." Danielle then began to reflect more on sharing and giving thanks. "And as a community of individuals we have so much more to share and to be thankful for. As a diversified people, we have so much to value. We need to better value our differences. We are all one earth. We are one people, unified on earth for greater community, for greater meaning. When Viktor Frankl shared with us Man's Search for Meaning, he gave us great insight on life from a concentration camp. We need to eliminate all prisons. Prisons are a major growth industry in our country, for both the public and private sectors. How unbelievable for us to contemplate that thought! What a statement for the greatest country on earth. How can we get the American people to realize what this truly means? Christ said 'whatever you do to the least of my brethren, that you do unto me!' Look what we are doing to our brothers and sisters who are in prison. Most of them come from poor backgrounds. A higher percentage of them are

minorities, representing some of the most beautiful colors of the rainbow. Can't we all just expend a fraction of what we earn and what we are worth to change this? Change this for the betterment of all people!"

"America is to be the model. Especially if it is the greatest country on earth. How can we help each child, man and woman to emulate better models? Each of us can be better than we are. How do we create that community of better people?"

"Don't we create it by focusing on each human relationship beginning with you and me? Like the song says, let it begin with me." Danielle also reflected on her relationship with her staff. "But we can also do it in work. By focusing on teams of people pursuing common goals. Making our teams more human, more compassionate. We need to realize we are talking about partnerships of people at every level within an organization and between organizations, true partnerships of people trying to create a greater community," Danielle offered.

"I think to accomplish this greater community among all people, in teams, in partnerships, in organizations and among organizations, we need to realize and cherish our individual value and differences. I believe that we need to better appreciate the feminine contribution, the nurturer in all of us. Perhaps it was my mother's influence, but I believe women and their skills and talents move the world. It would be interesting to reflect on how the world would be if we had women in power throughout the earth. Like in the Mideast and in Southeast Asia and India. Can you imagine the differences that would exist? Would we have the wars, the economic and human challenges, the differences between rich and poor? I believe not."

"Well Robert, I would like to agree with you, but I don't know. I know some beautiful women like my own mother as well as your mother. And yes they would make a significant difference, they already have. I also know and work with some wonderful women and work daily on women's health issues. But it is a human quality we are talking about. Yes there is value in femininity and the contributions of women. But we are talking about anyone who can unify the men and women of this earth. Any one who creates greater community among people, be it a political or corporate leader, teacher, principal, non-profit leader, or coach. Sometimes I think we all need to be better coaches," Danielle said.

"You are right. We need to focus on cooperation, collaboration and teams to make everything and everyone a little better."

"It has been my experience that if we focus on this cooperation, collaboration and teams, we become more tolerant of ourselves and others. Tolerance is a virtue. Although, when Christ overturned the table in the temple he seemed a bit intolerant."

"I think tolerance encompasses intolerance." Robert stated.

"If you think that respecting differences is another way of saying tolerance. Because I can understand someone respecting differences of people and being allowed to voice a difference, maybe even express an initial anger, as long as one returns to an equilibrium of tolerance or respect."

"A sort of transcendental acceptance."

"A place or state of being where we allow the other to be. We listen, empathize."

"Well Danielle, that is key. To listen. To really listen to the other. To allow them full expression. To truly listen to all that they say. Let them complete their thoughts and feelings. People express and want to express so much. Yet we are limited by time, pressure, and competing forces. With moments of silence and reflection in between."

Danielle let Robert complete his expression and she became more conscious of the need for the silence in between. "We often don't allow the silences in between. We interrupt sometimes in the midst of someone's thought. We have our own thoughts and we want to express them. But how important are they? How meaningful are each of our thoughts? Can you imagine how much better off we might be if we considered the value of our thoughts before we spoke them?"

Danielle had spent a lot of time during this vacation thinking about the value of her being, the value of her human contribution on this earth, to Robert, to Senator Hart to everyone she knew. She also thought about who she should spend time with. She had spent quality time with Robert this vacation. And both enjoyed it. There was a lot of time to talk, to listen, to just be with one another. Each was so busy back in Washington, D.C. with their professional lives, it had been quite a while since they had concentrated time with each other. And it was refreshing, renewing.

"This was so self-renewing, so refreshing, this time with you," Robert said.

"That's amazing. I was just thinking the same thing. It is like we are traveling on the same river of thought. I feel renewed and refreshed as well."

"This vacation was so empowering, to find and share ourselves again. With our independent yet shared life, we were able to appreciate and grow in the process," said Robert.

"Yes, we were able to realize our independence yet integrate the interdependence of our consciously decided married life."

"I like that phrase, consciously decided married life. I am not so sure how many married couples consciously decide to renew their married life together. We all need to do that more often," Robert expressed.

"You know, it is ironic. Although we are very married, there was real freedom to this vacation. Each of us freely did what we wanted, when we wanted. Yet, we did much together and enjoyed that as well."

"Freedom is an interesting concept. Freedom, like tolerance, seems to encompass its opposite. In our married life, some would think anyone married is never free, yet it allowed you and me to become who we are. We found our own freedom within. I don't think we ever felt constrained by this marriage. Or if we did, it was never expressed."

"It was like meeting all the wonderful people we met and shared time with this vacation. There were many people we might never imagine meeting, yet each contributed to us, and we to them, some in deeper ways than others."

Robert immediately thought of Bailey, as did Danielle.

"But it is in our openness, and I guess our freedom, to allow others into our lives, and we into theirs. Our freedom and openness to the moment and to other people is what brings human creativity to our lives. It creates new music, new scenes, new relationships, and new babies." Robert looked glowingly at Danielle.

She returned the warm feeling and felt the new life within. She was grateful for the new baby and for Robert.

Chapter 10
Create Legacy

It was Monday. Both Danielle and Robert returned to their work.

They felt reinvigorated, better able to do the good work they usually did. But a distinct change had occurred. As much as their lives were expanded by time spent alone and with each other, their thought processes and feelings had changed in ways they had never imagined. Here were two successful, imaginative and driven people leading fulfilling personal and professional lives in the nation's capital. What would their legacy be and what would their love be? Would they create a legacy of love?

Danielle was thinking about and feeling her baby. The new life within that she had never experienced before. Here was an experienced woman of the world, accomplished in a man's world, in the ultimate man's town, Washington, D.C., the seat of domestic and international power. But now like the blessed mother, she was feeling that life within, unique to childbearing age women who re-experience the ultimate giving, the ultimate nourishing, the ultimate love, giving birth to another unique human being. A human being with body and soul, who will need physical, financial, mental, social, community and spiritual guidance and help along the way.

That was the path she had chosen consciously with the man she married, loved, respected and united with many years before. On their most loving, refreshing and fulfilling vacation, they had made love and given life to the fortunate fetus within her sacred body. She was elated.

At the same time when she returned to work that Monday morning, she warmly and assertively embraced her small staff and the work before her. They were glad to have their boss, their leader, their inspiration back. She was glad to be back though she had thoroughly enjoyed her time away.

It was also the most complex time in her life. Not only with Robert. Not only with her new baby. Not only with her workers and her work. On this beautiful morning, Danielle was also thinking of Senator Hart and when she would see him next.

Here was the fortunate Danielle, greatly loved by Robert, a world renowned cardiologist, giving inspiration to their baby, and here she was in a successful professional position in a successful career, and yet she was thinking of her other lover, the distinguished Senator William Hart.

My God, my God, she reflected. She laughed a little to herself, how can all this be? Am I the most blessed woman on earth at the present time, or am I the most confused? I and Robert have been preoccupied by love, most conscious of love individually and collectively together, analyzing it, realizing it and feeling it in a multi-dimensional way and then I complicate it by the thought of Senator Hart. I so love and respect Senator Hart, as I, in a somewhat different way, love and respect Robert. How can this be? How can this be?

It just is, she proclaimed. It just is.

The issue now is, what do I do about it? How do I pursue it? It is so crazy. I must be so crazy. But in an odd way I feel fortunate, I feel blessed to know intimately two wonderful men who are doing so much for so many others.

Danielle realized she was at another crossroads in her life. She had made a conscious yet passionate decision to have a baby with Robert, a man she enjoyed, revered and loved. At the same time when alone, she longed for Senator Hart. Could she manage both love affairs? Would she want to balance both love affairs six months or a year from now? She thought so. She thought she had the best of both worlds. Perhaps it was characteristic of the American life, always competitive. What would it be like in America without competition? At times it seemed that competition was maximized in America through corporate competition, political competition and sports. In fact the central place sports had in America, even at the amateur and young age levels, was a marvel, from football in Texas, basketball in Indiana, girls basketball in Iowa, soccer up and down the East Coast, and little league baseball across the U.S. At the same time professional sports seemed, at times, to be out of control. The current National Basketball Association lockout threatened the continuation of organized professional basketball, of many multi-million dollar athletes who would never otherwise make that kind of money. Danielle wondered if her love life with Robert and Senator Hart was as out of control as the N.B.A. Could her life be more complicated? Was there a third lover out there or was she already too reckless?

Danielle had never been characterized as reckless. She had always been considered the most responsible woman. But now in her late thirties she was judged reckless, at least in her own mind and by society. A society rocked by sexual scandals at the highest levels of the private sector and government, threatening the very fabric of American life. England had faced this in the past. So had other countries. But never at the level of impact as the United States was being hit. Was it the beginning of the fall, especially with rising terrorist threats?

Danielle was reflecting now most seriously, most intensely on her own responsibility. She had always worked hard at school, been disciplined at work striving to achieve her own personal best. By most women's standards, even by men's standards, Danielle had achieved much. She was highly respected among women, her peers and other leaders in Washington, D.C. and in America who were involved in health issues. She had earned respect among various Administration officials under different political regimes and political parties in the White House. And similarly on the Hill, among Senators, House Representatives and their staff, especially chiefs of staff, legislative directors and the health staffs. Even her political opponents or adversaries on the Hill respected her for her work and her well considered positions.

But now Danielle was truly challenged within, by the presence of the growing fetus, her growing love for Robert, and her ever present love affair with Senator Hart.

She had worked so hard for her leadership position in health, in women's health, and in Washington circles including the Women in Government group. She was most responsible in her stewardship of women's health issues. Carefully articulating, positioning, and timing her minority opinion, which grew now into a majority opinion in health circles. When was America going to appropriately dedicate enough resources to women's, children's and elderly issues, and especially elderly women's issues? For over two decades, Washington's leaders had been paying lip service to women's issues, especially elderly women's issues. Congress with the support of the Administration had whacked $115 billion out of Medicare, with its biggest impact on elderly and disabled women. How could $115 billion be taken out of America's Medicare budget without having a negative impact on people? Ridiculous! Even with Government's claims of fraud, waste and abuse, most of which they were responsible for, there were significant dollars taken out of Medicare, America's leading program in the world for elderly and the disabled, most of whom were women. Why wasn't the health of America's women, who were the primary nurturers of America's children and America's workers, valued? This is what Danielle had been about.

But now, for the first time, Danielle had thought about her own legacy. Her legacy had never been part of her personal vocabulary. But now it was. Would her legacy be one of responsible health leader in America, especially for women's issues, a lover of life, human life and an advocate for equity among all people in realizing life's resources and human achievement potential? Or would she be known for her shadow?

Her shadow was characterized by a dual life, her daily life with Robert and a periodic one with Senator Hart, though his presence was also with her daily. Danielle had always been known for her thoughtfulness. If Danielle had done something wrong in the past, she had owned up to it in some way. She always cleaned up her messes since she was a little girl. Danielle had taken pride and made great effort to master her life. Self-mastery was an art as well as science for Danielle. Danielle had become so good in self-mastery, she was a role model for others. Responsibility was at the top of her characteristics, her virtues. But now, perhaps for the first time, she felt challenged, maybe even threatened, as she faced who she truly was. Plus, in nine months she would become a role model and nurturer for a baby girl or boy. What was she going to teach them? Danielle wasn't terrified by the thought, at least not yet.

All of a sudden the thought became bigger than life. Was Danielle responsible or not? To be a true lover, one needed to be a responsible lover. True self-mastery, true responsibility was not a one time or a sometime thing, Danielle thought. She had always been responsible, been known by others to be responsible. But now she was wrestling with a perspective on responsibility, a perspective on self-mastery she had never known. Only she and

Senator Hart knew this shadow side. Did her self-mastered responsibility have a deformed or deficient foundation? By most people's standards, yes. It now seemed like an uphill fight, at least a most perplexing puzzle that Danielle was almost afraid to figure out. Or had she figured it out and rationalized? What was she going to do? Give birth to Robert's baby in the coming year? And then Senator Hart's in the following year? A bizarre thought. Danielle had never had such thoughts. My God, how could I have gotten myself into such a predicament? I have no regrets about Robert's baby. Would I have no regrets about Senator Hart's baby? Robert would have some regrets about me having Senator Hart's baby. Or would he? How could he not, Danielle thought. Would Robert have to know the second baby was Senator Hart's? Would Senator Hart have to know it was his baby? Surely he would, but if he knew then Robert would know. At a minimum, I would know. I think I would, just like I knew I was having Robert's baby. I would surely know I was having Senator Hart's baby. This is so crazy, I have just learned I am having Robert's baby, and I am anticipating a baby with Senator Hart almost two years away. This is crazy, Danielle thought.

She then began to think deeply about love, her love for each of the two men, and her legacy. Her legacy. She had never really thought about it. But isn't that what life is truly about? One person's legacy, a family's legacy. A community's legacy. A nation's legacy. At this point it was challenging enough for Danielle to think about her own legacy. She would have to give some thought to their legacy.

What would Danielle be remembered for? In some ways she had created memories for herself and for others. She had never really thought of her own memories. Memories were for the elderly to reminisce. Although young people had memories too.

Perhaps of birthdays, their high school prom, graduations, even elementary and high schools.

For Danielle there were memories of her early life, but nothing regarding her legacy. She laughed at herself. Perhaps there was the legacy of her as a star basketball guard, quick, agile, determined, talented. Similarly there was her soccer prowess. In both she had been a state champion, an active participant on a winning state championship team. But Danielle was as proud of her scholastic achievements in high school that permitted her a great college education and earned her a master's degree in the fine arts as well as a master's in business administration.

But these were not what true legacies, meaningful legacies, were made of. There were other characteristics in her life that were the essence of legacies. She inherited much from her parents. Each of them had meaningful legacies! Their legacies were of love. They had devoted considerable time to their children and to each other. Danielle's sisters were very good people. Maria, her older sister, had a master's degree and taught elementary education. She had two wonderful teenage daughters who were succeeding in traditional DiCarlo fashion. The women in the family were beautiful, bright, talented and loving people. It must have been a mixture of Irish and Italian blood with a pinch of Spanish and French.

But Danielle, now reflecting on her fortunate genes with deep gratitude began to focus on legacy and on love. Was her legacy going to be a legacy of love? Or were the two distinct for her? Danielle was both perplexed and intrigued by the concepts, legacy and love, or a legacy of love. How distinct would her life be? In fact the longer Danielle focused on the issue, the more she was intrigued and intellectually and passionately fascinated about the true meaning of her life.

Not since her philosophy and psychology days in college and graduate school had she reflected on these questions.

Danielle was always known as an intense as well as fun-loving individual. As she grew older she became more intense, more intellectual, more goal-oriented and focused. But wasn't she as playful with Robert and Senator Hart? Remember the spilled ice cream on his lap? And there were other memories. Sitting on the Capitol steps looking west at midnight with a full moon. Picnics in isolated parks around Washington, D.C. Those light moments. Light but intense. Playful yes, but most serious too. As serious as one can get in life.

Danielle was reflecting on the loves of her life. Robert. Senator Hart. Her new baby. Her work, her avocation. Her colleagues and peers. Her staff. Her admirers. And those she admired, respected and loved.

Loved.

What does it mean, really mean to love and be loved? She reflected deeply on the elements of love she had so studied and analyzed and then tried to live in her own life.

How nurturing and supportive, how compassionate was she? Had she been? Was she going to be? Is she now? She thought of that which came naturally to her. Surely she had loved and nurtured, and was highly supportive of Robert. She had great compassion, empathy and passion for Robert. They loved to kiss, kiss passionately, hug and cuddle for hours. And then there was Senator Hart, an elected official of the U.S. Senate, revered by colleagues, and constituents, who felt strongly about representing their interests and representing the interests of those who needed him most, the minorities, the elderly, the disabled, the disenfranchised, the poor. Senator Hart was a leader among men and women. Be it the U.S. Senate or the world. Senator Hart had earned international plaudits and awards in Africa, the Far East, the Middle East and Europe for his humanitarian efforts. But as Danielle reflected on his meritorious life, she thought no less of Robert, the man she loved and married. Robert had accomplished much in his life in cardiology, domestically and internationally. And because of his research, his practice, his teaching he had touched many lives, many hearts in the United States and throughout the world. His research was world-renowned. His students were in countries throughout the world, practicing, teaching and researching. His talents had multiplied, like the loaves and the fishes.

Danielle thought she was so lucky, so fortunate to know intimately two men who had left an indelible mark on people, on the world. And generations, henceforth, would reap the benefits.

And then there was Danielle a beautiful talented person entwined with both men, complicating their lives and her own. Would her relationship with each man impact their legacy? It could she thought. She considered her relationship with each man. Her torrid love for and with each man. She loved each man dearly, she thought. But what if Robert knew? Wouldn't he be crushed? Or would he be understanding?

She had shared much with both. But something different with each man. She had spent much active passionate time with each man, listening, communicating and understanding.

Her challenge, her love challenge was how much truth she shared with each man? Hadn't she compartmentalized her relationship with each man? Was this her idea of control? Trying to control love.

Danielle recognized, appreciated and tried to live the truth. But was she? Would she live the truth? She tried to practice veracity in all thought and action. But she wasn't doing it. She couldn't do it. She was human. She had the potential to practice veracity in all thought and action. But what did that mean? Did it mean that she would be more truthful to herself, to the world, if she was truthful with either Robert or Senator Hart? Or could she complicate it even more if there were a third man? What was truth in this instance, denial of the thought, denial or sacrifice of the relationship with either man? This truly was the ultimate perplexity for Danielle. No matter how hard she tried she was caught in a world where there seemed to be no black or white. But she knew deep down there was black and white. And there was gray and blue and yellow and passionate red. And all the colors in the rainbow. In her rainbow.

Danielle would continue to focus on being true, on being more sincere. She would continue to learn what integrity in her life meant. It was not a legal definition. It was an authentic definition she sought. She would learn to recognize, appreciate and live the truth in her life. The question was how. The answer was unknown.

When Danielle thought about the fairness, equity and even-handedness of love, she realized in her professional life this was a driving principle. In her private life, it was perplexing. In her own mind she was being as fair, equitable and even-handed as she could be, with herself and her lovers. This principle dominated her professional career and daily life especially towards women and different people and races.

Regarding respect for life, Danielle thought she focused as much as anyone on sustaining life in all its forms. She had been active in protecting the environment. She treasured friendship with many different people. She was a decent person. She said thanks often and for many things. There was a grace that she carried with her, that she conveyed to others that reflected her respect for life. The only thing that troubled her, but not greatly, was the element of sorrow, of being sorry, of saying she was sorry. She recognized it might be a gift. It was a powerful and meaningful dimension of life. She would be sorry to lose her mother and father. And her sisters. If and when they left this earth.

She wondered greatly if she would be able to say she was sorry to either Robert or Senator Hart. She hoped, perhaps arrogantly, that she would never have to. Danielle, like Bobby Kennedy, thought the impossible, because they lived the impossible until they died. Perhaps that would be her legacy, she dreamt and lived the impossible life. One envied by many.

That was not her conscious life or legacy. She wondered what was her legacy.

Another aspect in Danielle's life was her love focus on unifying and embracing all peoples of the world, now and in the future in a cooperative and participative global community. The challenge was how to appropriately connect and maximize this high touch, high technology world, especially in a time when there were such vast differences in available resources. Danielle believed in unifying people, valuing their differences, building on those differences and unique contributions. Danielle was team-oriented in all that she did. But how was she team-oriented when one considered the team of three, Danielle, Robert and Senator Hart. An odd or cohesive team?

Danielle was strong and optimistic about partnerships. Even a partnership of odd bedfellows. Like public/private partnerships, those that would transcend most people's imagination or common sense.

Danielle had great tolerance but she respected the story of Christ who expressed a lack of tolerance when he upended the table in the temple. Danielle expressed her tolerance in many ways. She had been part of several different cultural presentations. She accepted a lot in life if it did not convey anything of injustice to human beings. There she would draw the line. Danielle had great empathy. She could listen, listen actively for long periods of time. She would allow others great freedom. But she expected the same. She especially thought this when she reflected about Robert and Senator Hart. She respected differences and she expected others to allow and respect those differences as well.

Speaking of freedom, Danielle fostered human creativity in every way she could, in her own life, and in the lives of others. It was something her mother and father fostered. Freedom of expression was of great value, in light of the many talents and potentials men and women possessed. Danielle's warm home was strong on aesthetics, from flowers to pictures and knick knacks. From the baby grand piano that all the girls played for years, to the plays and songs that were rehearsed and played out in her home as a child and teenager. Later as adults, Danielle and her sisters enjoyed holidays and celebrations by singing, dancing, piano and guitar playing in their parent's home.

Danielle, like Robert and Senator Hart, all put high premiums on self renewal in their lives. It allowed them to excel in their professional lives. In each of their lives there was a high premium on independence, yet an equal value on community and interdependence. For Robert, the community of cardiologists, practitioners, researchers and teachers. For Senator Hart, with the other 99 Senators, former Senators and all elected officials. Yet with both there was strong allegiance and connection to those they served, patients and constituents.

For Danielle, she realized satisfactions in many communities of health providers, health advocates and consumers especially women, children and the elderly.

There was a self-evident courage in their lives that propelled Danielle, Robert and Senator Hart to do more good. They had accomplished much and there was much more good to do.

Danielle thought that people did not utilize the courage within themselves to do a lot more good than they were doing already.

She was thinking that she, Robert and Senator Hart realized this and the more they realized it the more they set the bar higher to accomplish potential good. All people realize this. They all thought this and so did their family and friends. Perhaps, she thought, if we created a new curricula on love and its attributes, responsibility, truthfulness, fairness, respect for life, unity, freedom and tolerance, we would accomplish much more good in the world. If we nurtured, celebrated, helped and served others more, we would realize the potential of love. Love would be our legacy. We would create more leaders. More leaders of love and all that it represents.

Such leaders of love would enrich life and create more wonder and awareness. The wonder and awareness of love.

Danielle hoped that people would become more gentle, flexible and fun loving. More gentle in love, more flexible with love and more fun in love. Learn love, renew love, contribute love and share love. Love, love, and love some more. Share and create a legacy of love.

* * *

On Monday, Robert had returned to all types of challenges. The combination of practice, teaching, and research demands that he faced that morning were almost overwhelming. His two-week hiatus created a backlog of patient visits. Add to that his part-time research schedule with several papers due, and a part-time teaching schedule. This class of incoming students was to be the best in years. So, it was to be a very busy few weeks. At the same time Robert was thinking of Danielle and what a great time they had on vacation. Probably the best one they had ever shared. And now she was expecting a new child next spring! They were both very excited. Robert realized that he had a fulfilling life at the present time. Demanding yet satisfying. He realized that he was loved and yet the demands on him were great. Robert had never thought about his legacy. But now faced with life as it was, he had great expectations for himself. There was much to do. This man of the heart had loved his life. Indeed he was feeling quite happy yet determined to bring more happiness to others, Danielle, his colleagues, his patients, his students, his peers and others he would encounter along the way.

At the same time, and on top of this fortunate state he was thinking about Bailey.

And Bailey was simultaneously thinking of him.

As Robert thought of her, he considered what a complicating yet beautiful thought it was. He did love Danielle and he believed she loved him as deeply. They had spent a wonderful time reflecting upon the principles of love, things like responsibility, truthfulness, respect for life, fairness, freedom, tolerance and the like. Robert was thinking hundreds of things simultaneously. Danielle, his cardiology challenges with patients, students, peers and staff. And thinking of Bailey. Thinking of Bailey with love and fondness.

Bailey was so extraordinary. Such a beautiful woman and a wonderful personality. And to think she was a cardiologist as well! It was so incredible to think that they shared so much in common. It was so easy and so coherent, so clear when we communicated, when we saw each other, visited with each other, laughed with each other, conversed and had dinner together. The verbal and the nonverbal communication was so real. She was truly a unique individual that I look forward to seeing again, he thought. And she expressed the same to me....

It will be easy for us to see each other at cardiology meetings. I can't believe that could happen often. Our feelings and intellectual connections seemed so strong when we talked. It was like we were on the same raft swiftly flowing down the river. A gorgeous river, like I imagine the Colorado river or any other great river of life.

Why am I so flowing with the thoughts and feelings of Bailey? So out of the ordinary, so extraordinary. Especially when I have Danielle, a magnificent woman in her own right.

And here I am a responsible cardiologist, a teacher and researcher whose mind is overtaken with the strength of another wonderful and magnificent woman.

What will I do with my life, with these women I love? My life has been so full of love and opportunities to love others. Through cardiology, through family and friends, through the Washington community. Through our international community of cardiology and our friends in Washington that Danielle and I know.

Our good fortune obviously came from our family originally.

A family or I dare say two families, and four families before that, as we look back to the generations before Danielle and me.

Those families were legacies of love. A love handed down

211

to us through the generations. A love we have been fortunate to get to know and cherish. It is the great bond of life. Love is the essence of life. An essence we have been fortunate to experience.

The challenges for people like Danielle and me, and Bailey, is what is our love, what is our legacy, and is our legacy a legacy of love or is it a legacy or love?

Obviously with the gifts we have been given and have developed, Danielle, Bailey and I have opportunities and responsibilities. The opportunities are to love even more and better than we have. How do we express it and nourish it? Is it an expanding love, the essence of life or is it something else?

I feel my love is at a crossroads. Not that it is headed down a path distant from myself. But my love is confused or complicated at best. I know I love Danielle but what form and path it will take is an unknown. It is like my research. I have hunches based on my experience and my past research. But to guess the outcome is a stretch.

It will be interesting to see how we handle our first child, in less than nine months. Will it be a boy or a girl? Will it bring Danielle and I closer together? One would think it would. I have heard often how the children become all-consuming for the mother. Because the woman is the initial nurturer that is to be expected. It consumes most of the mother's time in the initial years. What impact will it have on Danielle and me? Our careers have consumed us. Will she merely transfer this time to our new child? Knowing Danielle, she may become a full-time mother for a while, but eventually she will need the fulfillment of her career.

I know Danielle. She will love the child, love me, love her health work and love whoever she encounters. She is just a loving person. And always will be a loving person. Her life is a legacy of love.

My challenge is to love like Danielle does. Or, I dare say, surpass Danielle's legacy as a lover.

And Bailey. What kind of lover is she? Not just physically, but mentally, socially, psychologically, spiritually, etc. My guess is she is the equal of Danielle. She is obviously bright, warm, personable, respected, thoughtful, trustworthy, all the characteristics of a great lover. Hers also is a legacy of love. I would love to know more about her legacy. I would like to know more about her as a person. As a lover.

That's an awesome thought? As I got to know Bailey how would that impact my life with Danielle and our new child? How would I be as a lover then? I would be tested as never before. I would be tested to the ultimate in all that I do.

As I sit here reflecting on Bailey, I reflect on what love really is, what it represents in my life and what it should be, as Danielle and I discussed during our vacation.

Those were great conversations. The kind of conversations people should have about life and love, which is at the heart of life.

Here I am, a man whose profession centers around the heart, facing the challenge of loving two beautiful women.

I take a deep breath, think of both women, Danielle and Bailey. And then I think I need to talk to someone. Perhaps Ben Davidson. Big Dr. Ben Davidson. The only cardiologist and psychiatrist I know well. An interesting guy. Tremendous dimension to him. Plus he is a philosopher and lover of life. Likes the good life. Good people. Good places. Good music and good wine. Ben is one of the earth's great people. I'll have to share with him my love predicament. But on second thought, I haven't engaged in much with Danielle. Maybe I need to second think this. Give myself a second opinion. But then again maybe I need to practice preventive cardiology. Sometimes it is difficult to get us trained and practicing cardiologists, especially if one is a researcher, to think enough of prevention.

But what am I preventing? Love between two people? Love between three people? Is it love at all? Is it anything at all? I want to call Bailey. Nothing wrong with that. But what do I say? What does she say?

We can talk about cardiology. We can talk about preventive cardiology. Or perhaps we will discuss the subjects of our legacy, our love or our legacy of love. But that would be presumptuous. Or would it? Isn't love presumptuous? We know ultimate love is unconditional. There was no doubt in my mind that attraction between Bailey and me was unmistakable. So was the passion we felt for each other. Because we are heart professionals we know enough about the organ to know the real thing when we see it, and feel it. And we did.

Robert decided the better part of valor and appropriateness was to wait another day to call Bailey. Think about it some more. See if Bailey would call him. And reflect on what he desired for his true legacy. Was it to be a legacy of love? And if so how would it play out? Robert knew that love was the ultimate in life. He also knew that the ultimate legacy was that of love. But who and how to love in his remaining life was the challenge, his challenge regarding legacy and love. Perhaps a legacy of love.

214

Epilogue

It was Sunday morning. Danielle attended mass at Mary Magdalene Church in Naples. As a Catholic whose family was very sensitive to religion and always valued the spiritual, Danielle relished the quiet haven of church, especially on this beautiful warm Sunday morning.

How ironic, she thought, appreciating the renowned life of Mary Magdalene. Danielle felt a little like Mary Magdalene. She had just given a talk to a women's health group on Saturday at the University of Miami. She was planning another talk at Florida Gulf Coast University. Danielle was conscious of her dual life, with Robert and Senator Hart.

How could she, how would she go on in this complicated, yet personally rewarding life? And how had she complicated that by becoming pregnant with Robert? It was a pregnancy she loved. And to think she had also dreamed of being pregnant by Senator Hart with her second child! How could she think such thoughts? It was part of the greatness of human life, to have the power to create any reality. This along with spiritual, emotional, psychological, social, economic and transcendent aspects of our being, allowed Danielle to enjoy her wonderful, always creative life.

Here she was in a moment of silence, alone reflecting upon her fulfilling life.

As she proceeded to Holy Communion, she felt surreal. She focused on the priest giving communion to one person after another as she proceeded up the aisle. She felt like Mary Magdalene as she reached the priest.

Upon receiving Holy Communion Danielle felt the spiritual exhilaration of the Holy Spirit move in her womb. She

215

felt a tingling sensation all over, the kind of tingling you felt when in the presence of someone greater than yourself, someone most overwhelming.

She remembered the words they had all repeated before communion began, "Lord, I am not worthy to receive you, but only say the word and I will be healed."

Heal me Lord, she thought. Heal me.

Heal me Lord and guide me. Help me. Make my legacy a legacy of love, as difficult as that may seem!

AFTERWORD

In the preface I outlined why I wrote the book. I also had some suggestions for you to think about regarding your loves, your legacy, perhaps a legacy of love.

I have more suggestions. And I solicit your suggestions.

First tell your story. Tell it to yourself. Make it as long as you like. Then go back and read it and retell it. Retell your story not only in terms of what has happened but what may and will happen in your life if it should last one hundred and twenty years. Ridiculous you may first comment, but it is very realistic in light of today's medical and health developments. Living to one hundred and twenty is even more realistic if you consciously want to live that long.

Your wants, desires, passions are what matter within the framework of a deeply reflective or contemplative life. That is what most of us are missing in this fast paced world of ours. There is fast company all around us. So take some time. You deserve it.

And tell your story.

First, some suggestions about writing your story of five to twenty pages. Or more if you like. Then remember you will read it, reflect on it, and revise it to find deeper meaning within you.

Try to determine the phases of your life. Oftentimes they may be linked to school (elementary, middle school, high school, college, graduate school). They may be linked to certain jobs, professions or careers. They could be linked to significant volunteer activities.

Then there are the loves in your life: mother, father, brother(s), sister(s), spouses, lovers, spouses who are lovers, grandparents, cousins, friends or significant others.

Certain homes, neighborhoods or cities you have lived in could be significant.

Is there lots of sun, water, mountains, rain, cold, heat, snow that is significant, positive or negative, for you?

But then really reflect on those loves in your life. Who or what are the significant loves or passions in your life? Money is critical. But you and I are looking for something much more significant than what money is or brings.

Focus on the loves and passions. Who are you really? Who can you be? Your life has great meaning. It has had great meaning, greater than you have realized. And it may and will have more meaning if you tell your story, reflect on it and focus on it. After all, you are most significant. It is your life and you can do what you want with it. Use the last few pages of this book to write those initial reflections on your loves, passions and legacy.

Next, after writing your life story, you need to see it in the context of looking back on your life, previewing that you have one death, one life, allowing for the fact that you may have been here before and may return again but not as you or others know you.

So assume you are dead and we are at your memorial service, the wake, the mass, the ceremony, whatever. Think of three people you would pick, who know you, who loved you in some way. What would they say about you?

218

What do you want them to say about you?

This is the question we want to focus on. Who you are and who you can be? Who do you want to be? You see be-ing is what it is all about.

So what do you want to realize, to be in your life? Dream you can be who you want to be and the odds are greater that it will happen. And others do too.

Search for love and legacy in your life.
Search for the legacy of love in your life.

You will be richer and more satisfied with your life. And others will be the beneficiaries and have more satisfied lives. Rich, in every way of our be-ing, and more satisfied. Isn't that what everyone wants? Peace and harmony realized through more legacies of love including most importantly, you.

As I contemplate my next writing, let me know how I can help you, your loves, your legacy, and your organization, whether family, corporation, association, affiliation or whatever. For your information, insight and pursuit, I have included various bibliography and references. These include my interpretation of key principles and ethical values as written and talked about by various well known authors who have written about love and its attributes.

Good luck on your legacy of love.

Bibliography

Bennett, William J. *The Book of Virtues.* Simon and Shuster, New York, 1996.

Blanchard, Ken and Vincent Peale. *The Power of Ethical Management.* William Morrow and Co. New York, 1988.

Buscaglia, Leo F. *Love.* Fawcett Book Group, New York, 1996.

Covey, Stephen R. *The Seven Habits of Highly Effective People.* Simon and Shuster, New York, 1990.

Foster, Rick and Greg Hicks, *How We Choose To Be Happy.* Putnam, New York, 1999.

Frankl, Viktor. *Man's Search For Meaning.* Beacon Press, Boston, 1959.

Fromm, Erich. *The Art of Loving.* Harper, New York, 1956.

Fulghum, Robert. *All I Really Needed to Know I Learned in Kindergarten.* Villard Books, 1988

Henderson, Hazel. *Paradigms in Progress: Life Beyond Economics.* Berrett-Koehler, San Francisco, 1995.

Kidder, Rushworth M. *Shared Values for a Troubled World: Conversations with Men and Women of Conscience.* Jossey-Bass Inc. Publishers, San Francisco, 1994.

Liebig, James. *Merchants of Vision: People Bringing New Purpose and Values to Business.* Berrett-Koehler Publishers Inc., San Francisco, 1994.

Peck, M. Scott. *The Road Less Traveled.* Simon and Shuster, New York, 1994.

Rosen, Robert H. *The Healthy Company.* Putnam Publishing Group, New York, 1992.

Senge, Peter. *The Fifth Discipline.* Doubleday, New York, 1989.

Teresa, Mother. *No Greater Love.* New World Library, Novato, California, 1997.

COUGHLAN	BENNETT	BLANCHARD/PEALE	BUSCAGLIA	COVEY
LEGACY OR LOVE	**BOOK OF VIRTUES**	**ETHICAL MANAGEMENT**	**LOVE**	**SEVEN HABITS**
Love	Compassion	How Will It Make Me Feel About Myself If Front Page If Family Knew	Love; Share; Create Joy; Touch Feel, Show Emotion	Put First Things First Most Important Dependence
Responsibility	Responsibility Self Discipline Hard Work		Responsibility	Take Responsibility For Our Attitudes and Actions
Truthfulness	Honesty	Is It Legal	Love Yourself	Understand Desired Direction
Fairness	Loyalty	Is it Balanced Is it Fair; Short Term And Long Term	Love Always Creates, Never Destroys	WIN/WIN Mutual Benefit Psychic Deposit
Respect for Life			Recognizes Needs: Self Respect, Self Love	
Unity	Friendship		Togetherness, Universal Love	Synergize Creatively Cooperate Value Differences
Freedom	Courage		Free Yourself of Labels; Be Free to Learn; Spontaneous	Self Renew Emotional, Physical, Mental, Spiritual Independence
Tolerance			Patient; Accepting Understanding; Say Yes to Differences	Seek First to Understand Empathy, Listening, Psychic

Explanatory Note: This is my interpretation of key words and phrases used by the respective authors relating to Love, Responsibility, Truthfulness, Fairness, Respect for Life, Unity, Freedom and Tolerance - William D. Coughlan

COMPARISON OF ETHICAL VALUES/PRINCIPLES				
FOSTER/HICKS	**FRANKL**	**FROMM**	**FULGHUM**	**KIDDER**
HOW TO BE HAPPY	**MAN'S SEARCH FOR MEANING**	**THE ART OF LOVING**	**KINDERGARTEN**	**SHARED VALUES**
Intention; Giving/ Sharing Happiness; Profound Enduring Feeling	Love; Ultimate and Highest Goal	Love	Share Everything	**Love**
Accountability	Responsible to Life: Responsibleness Meaning of Sacrifice	Motherly Love; Love Between Parent and Child	Put Things Back Where You Found Them, Clean Up Your Own Mess	**Responsibility**
Truthfulness; Honest	Truth; Absolute Honesty	Self Love; Know Thyself	Don't Take Things That Aren't Yours	**Truthfulness**
Identification		Brotherly Love; Collaboration	Play Fair	**Fairness**
Appreciation Live in Moment	Spiritual Being	Respect; Love of God	Say You're Sorry When You Hurt Somebody	**Respect for Life**
Centrality; Integrated	Central Position - Affording Protection	Feels One with Nature	When You Go Out Into The World, Watch Out for Traffic, Hold Hands & Stick Together	**Unity**
Options: Flexible, Open	Freedom to Choose Spiritual Freedom Freedom from Suffering	Love is the Child of Freedom Erotic Love	Live a Balanced Life	**Freedom**
Recasting Reframe	Humor - Rise Above Bear Suffering	Mutual Tolerance Team spirit; Patience	Don't Hit People	**Tolerance**

Explanatory Note: This is my interpretation of key words and phrases used by the respective authors relating to Love, Responsibility, Truthfulness, Fairness, Respect for Life, Unity, Freedom and Tolerance - William D. Coughlan

COMPARISON OF ETHICAL VALUES/PRINCIPLES				
LIEBIG	MOORE	PECK	ROSEN	SENGE
MERCHANTS OF VISION	CARE OF THE SOUL	ROAD LESS TRAVELED	HEALTHY COMPANY	FIFTH DISCIPLINE
Celebrate Common Good Fortune, Nurture Heart and Spirit	Love	Love	Power and Influence	
Leadership & Responsibility Stewardship Responsible to the Whole	Soulful Responsibility	Discipline	Be a Helper, Serve Passion for Products and Process	Personal Mastery
Integrity Behave Authentically Truth, Dialectical and Paradoxical	Conversation/Letters	Withholding Truth Black and White Lies	Commitment to Self Knowledge and Development Trust, Honest	Continuing Learning
Enhance Social Equity	Endings The Future of Former Relationships		Appreciation for Flexibility/Resilience	Structure Channel Energy
Protect the Natural Environment Sustain Life	The Sacred Friendship Spirituality Holiness of Sex	Religion/Grace	Firm Belief in Decency	
Serve Higher Purposes Community Cooperate, Relate	Intimacy Family Community Intermingled Souls Grace	Grace	Spirit of Partnership Build Relationships	Teams
Foster Human Creativity	Intimate Imagination Attachment Individuality Bonding and Bondage	Escape from Freedom Love is Separateness The Risk of Independence	High Priority for Health and Well-being	Leader-Build Shared Vision Empower, Redesign
Cultural Preservation Transcendental Acceptance	Allow Some Uncertainty		Respect for Individual Differences	

Explanatory Note: This is my interpretation of key words and phrases used by the respective authors relating to Love, Responsibility, Truthfulness, Fairness, Respect for Life, Unity, Freedom and Tolerance - William D. Coughlan

	LONG VIEW (EMERGING VALUES)	**SHORT VIEW (PEAKING OF OLD VALUES)**
Love	Qualitative	Quantitative
Truthfulness	Concern and debate over ethics, values	"Business as usual," "Economicism" has won
Fairness	New indicators of development for major social trends geared to provide feedback to social goals Increase savings rates, balance budget Globalizing education Reducing arms budgets	Gross national product and macro economics Debt financing, credit cards Addictive society and organizations Program trading "futures," options, etc.
Freedom	Shopping guides for a better world Systemic reconceptualizing and redesign Rise of green parties and movements	"Lifestyles of the rich and famous" Technological "fixes" Low environmental concern
Unity	Integrative "Macro-rigorous" concern for community cooperation Participatory partnership	Reductionist," Micro-rigorous" Greed, individualistic, competitive Hierarchical, dominator
Tolerance	Government priorities in negotiations Conflict resolution "Green" levies and user fees	Government priorities in armaments, hardware Tax code subsidizes resource depletion
Responsibility	Socially responsible investing "Eco-labeled" products Pro-active, preventive, problem-identification	Speculation, paper asset shuffling Advertising geared to infantile desire Crisis model of problem-solving, "Band-aid" remedies
Respect for Life	Investing in people: the new "Wealth of Nations" Frugality, search for inner satisfactions and personal growth.	Budget and trade deficits, international debt Consumption values and addictions

Source: Hazel Henderson,
Paradigms in Progress, 1995
Life Beyond Economics, P. 80, Berrett-Koehler Publishers, San Francisco

Explanatory Note: This is my interpretation of Hazel Henderson's Emerging Values and Old Values as related to Love, Truthfulness, Fairness, Freedom, Unity, Tolerance, Responsibility and Respect for Life - William D. Coughlan

Great Example of Legacy of Love: Mother Teresa

Perhaps the greatest example of a legacy of love in the twentieth century was Mother Teresa. She created over six hundred houses to assist the poor and disabled in over one hundred and thirty countries and still had no debt. She won the Nobel Peace Prize in Oslo and numerous international awards. The U.N. General Secretary called her the most powerful woman in the world. She was called a living saint.

Among her many writings, No Greater Love contains the most accessible and most inspirational gathering of her thoughts.

"Give of your hands to serve and your hearts to love."

"The more disgusting the work, the greater love must be, as it takes succor to the Lord disguised in the rags of the poor."

"If we really want to love, we must first learn to forgive before anything else."

"People who really and truly love each other are the happiest people on earth."

"The fruit of love is service."

"Give free service to the poor."

"Let us interweave our lives with bonds of sacrifice and love, and it will be possible for us to conquer the world."

"Start by loving one another within our families."

"True love is love that causes us pain, that hurts, and yet brings us joy. We must pray to God and ask him to give the courage to love."

"Realize this love through meditation, the spirit of prayer, and sacrifice, by an intense interior life."

"What is required of a Missionary of Charity is this: health of mind and body, ability to learn, a good dose of good sense and a joyous character."

"God loves me, I'm not here just to fill a place, just to be a number. He has chosen me for a purpose. I knew it."

BIOGRAPHY

Bill Coughlan is a writer, speaker, facilitator, visionary, strategist, mentor and consultant in life, leadership and management issues and topics.

He has provided leadership in the national association world for over 23 years. He served for over four years as President and CEO for the National Association of Medical Equipment Services, seven years as the CEO for the American Physical Therapy Association and seven years as Deputy Executive Vice President for the American College of Cardiology. Previous employment was with the American College of Physicians in Philadelphia, and the American Medical Association in Chicago. He also worked for CNA in Chicago. He is a fellow of the American Society of Association Executives and has served on their Board of Directors. He also served on the Board of Directors of the Professional Convention Management Association and received their President's Award for Community Service. He was active in the Greater Washington Society of Association Executives and chaired their CEO and Government Relations Committees.

Bill has also managed and served in the Federal Department of Health and Human Services for five years as a civil servant in the offices of the Secretary and the Assistant Secretary of Health. He has also been a locally elected official, serving as Chairman of the Columbia Council, in Columbia, Maryland, one of his three homes. He has a home and residence in Arrowhead at Vail, Colorado and spends part of the year in Naples, Florida.

Bill Coughlan is a fifty four year old grandfather of three and father of six children - ages 26-33. He has been told he doesn't look his age.

Some of his enlightenment has come through his graduate work, which has resulted in Masters Degrees in Philosophy from DePaul University, as well as Health Administration Environmental Science from Governors State University and Public Administration from the University of Southern California.

226

QUICK ORDER FORM
Tear out and fax to:
Coughlan and Associates
301-596-1553
Telephone Orders: 877-850-4938
E-mail orders: wcoughlan@home.com
Postal orders: Coughlan and Associates
P.O. Box 6625
Columbia, MD 21045
Please call or send me more information on: (check applicable)
_____ Speeches
_____ Individual Facilitation/Consulting
_____ Group Facilitation/Retreat

Special offer:
I would like _____ additional copies of Legacy or Love, personally autographed by the author
at $15 each USA _____
at $23 each Canada _____
USA add $4 shipping 1st book, $2 each add'l book
Canada add $9 shipping 1st book, $5 each add'l book
Name:
Address:
City:
Telephone:
E-mail address:
Payment:___Check___Credit card:
___Visa___Mastercard___Discover___Amex
Name on Card:
Card Number: Exp. Date_____

Legacy or Love Notes

Legacy or Love Notes

Legacy or Love Notes